The Mystery of the Scarlet Homes of Sherlock

The Lost Diaries of Sir Arthur Conan Doyle, Vol. 1

I0628316

Edited by

PROF. RICHARD KREVOLIN

&

DR. JOHN RAFFENSPERGER

Paperback ISBN 978-1-78092-968-2
ePub ISBN 978-1-78092-969-9
PDF ISBN 978-1-78092-970-5

Published in the UK by MX Publishing
335 Princess Park Manor, Royal Drive,
London, N11 3GX
www.mxpublishing.co.uk

Cover design by Brian Belanger

To our esteemed editor, Nancy Cohen, our wonderful agent, Paula Munier, Renee Braeunig, Melanie Jappy, Kathy Copas, Colleen Sell, Dr. Wally Duff, Dr. Glenn Shepard, John Haslett, Penny Macleod, Steve Callender, Katja Bressette, Katia Haddidian, Coach Bob Orgovan, and the Sanibel writing group four.

I have always been a collector of Sherlockiana and a medical history scholar. As a result, when I heard that a trunk of Sir Arthur Conan Doyle's personal effects—which had been willed to J.M. Barrie and held by his estate for almost eighty years—was finally coming up for auction at Sotheby's, I eagerly placed a bid. Luck was on my side, and I was fortunate to win the old footlocker from the estate of Sir Arthur Conan Doyle's dear friend and classmate at the University of Edinburgh who created Peter Pan.

I hauled the heavy treasure home and opened it in the living room of my little apartment. But, all that was inside was a smelly bunch of old, heavy wool blankets and rusted medical instruments. I felt like a fool for spending so much money on a bunch of trash.

As I was about to close up the chest on yet another disappointing purchase related to my obsession with Sherlock Holmes, I took time for a closer look, just to be sure. It was then that I noticed a little compartment on the inside of the lid of the footlocker. I slipped my hand in and, to my astonishment, pulled out three leather-bound, hand-written journals.

Stunned, I sat down in my kitchen and cracked open the first one. A folded piece of paper and a lock of red hair fell out. I smoothed out the yellowing paper and was shocked when I read:

It is July 7, 1930. I am gravely ill and do not think I will live through the night. And so, it has become incumbent upon me to deal with these treasured journals from my medical-school days that reveal the most personal details of the formative moments of my young life.

Due to their private nature, I thought it would be unseemly if they outlived me. An hour ago I walked them over to the fireplace in my library determined to burn them. But, when the heat of the flames licked their spines, I rescued them, like a mother hen grabbing her ducklings just before a waterfall.

Instead, despite some reluctance, I will place these journals in my old footlocker and ensure they are well-hidden. A message in a bottle that, perhaps, will someday be discovered by one who has learned the powers of careful observation . . . Or will be left, unnoticed, to disintegrate over the years.

~ Sir Arthur Conan Doyle

And so, almost one hundred years later, with the publication of this volume, Sir Arthur Conan Doyle's dying choice to recover his journals so that they might one day see light is now being justified in these pages. You, dear reader, hold the first of the "lost" diaries of Sir Arthur Conan Doyle, written in 1878 while he was a nineteen-year-old student at the University of Edinburgh Medical School.

This volume details the story of Doyle's first year of service as the clerk for Dr. Joseph Bell, as well as shedding light on the origin of many of Robert Louis Stevenson and J. M. Barrie's most famous characters.

I now entrust this diary to you, my dear reader. I hope you gain as much pleasure perusing its pages as I did when I first discovered it buried deep within the wooden confines of that ancient treasure chest...

~ Dr. John Raffensperger, Sanibel Island, Florida, 7:56 a.m. February 29, 2016.

25 September, 1878

"Mr. Doyle, for heaven's sake, open your eyes and mind! Observe, deduce, and connect. Employ your faculties of reason, however limited they may be. The tiniest of details might be the key to reaching a proper diagnosis and saving a life. Otherwise, abandon a career in medicine, try your hand at writing and see how well that goes."

I squeezed my hands into fists and tried to blot out the professor's taunts from my mind. Dr. Bell is utterly maddening. He was riding me hard just because earlier in the day I had misdiagnosed a hernia in a squalling baby. There are many times I would gladly plunge a scalpel into his heart—that is if he had one.

I didn't think it was humorous, but, as Bell's pretentious, willowy voice subsided, my classmate's giggles grew into howls of laughter and the stomping of feet. Damn them all for having fun at my expense!

Let me explain. It was late afternoon and uncomfortably hot in the amphitheatre of the Royal Edinburgh Infirmary—too hot for my wool suit. Ah, if I only owned another lighter one I would be wearing it, but alas, as a poor medical student it was all I had . . .

I was fulfilling my responsibilities as Dr. Joseph Bell's outpatient clerk, tasked with examining his patients to arrive at a tentative diagnosis before he discussed the case in front of a class of medical students. I had been chosen to replace his former student clerk, my mate John Watson, when he decided to leave university and enter the military.

The great amphitheatre was packed with students and still had the stench of carbolic and chloroform from the morning's operations. I was in the anteroom with the last of the day's nearly fifty patients. He was a huge brute of a man around forty with a long, red beard that barely hid a hard, pocked face. His shoulders and muscular biceps bulged through a thick woolen shirt, and his black, homespun pants were stuck into mud-stained, cowhide, knee-high boots. He slurred his words and walked with a shuffling gait.

"Your name, please," I asked.

"MacLure."

"What's the matter?"

"It's me fingers," he said.

"Well, what about your fingers?"

"See for yourself."

Before my very eyes, he held up his right hand. The fourth and fifth fingers turned from a deathly white to blue and then to a dull red color. I had never before seen, nor read about, anything like that dramatic color change.

"Mr. Doyle, my next patient, if you please," Dr. Bell called.

I led Mr. MacLure into the amphitheatre, fully expecting Dr. Bell to ridicule my findings.

Dr. Bell cleared his throat. "Mr. Doyle, you have examined the patient, aye?" he asked.

"Aye."

"We eagerly await your diagnosis."

"From the patient's shuffling gait and slurred speech, he appears to be under the influence of strong drink."

"You observe nothing else?"

"Um, well, well . . . It's his fingers. They change color."

"Is that all?"

"That is quite serious, is it not, sir?"

"You noted nothing else?"

"Nothing, sir."

"What about the tobacco stains on his beard and the ulcer on the top of his right ear?" Bell asked.

I looked at my feet while a classmate chortled. "I don't know, but can't see that they have any connection to his illness."

And this was the moment he made that oh so humiliating statement, "Mr. Doyle, for heaven's sake, open your eyes and mind! Observe, deduce, and connect. Employ your faculties of reason, however limited they may be. The tiniest of details might be the key to reaching a proper diagnosis and saving a life. Otherwise, abandon a career in medicine, try your hand at writing and see how well that goes."

Dammit all! How can I be so dense? Dr. Bell and I can gaze at the same patient and yet, somehow, he always seems to notice minute details that I miss and draw conclusions that I can never reach.

"I don't see how a tobacco stain can—" I countered. Before I could finish Dr. Bell cleared his throat. "Laddie, sometimes I wonder if you have the cerebral facility for a future in the medical arts."

His words stung. I blushed, but did not defend myself. My job as clerk is to make an initial appraisal of the patients. Once again, I had failed miserably . . .

"Please tell us, sir. How do the ulcer and tobacco stains relate to his medical condition?" I asked.

"The ulcer is undoubtedly the result of an old case of frostbite, and tobacco aggravates this disease." Bell rose from his chair. "Doyle, please return to your seat and let me question this man further."

I hung my head and stumbled to my place in the front row of students.

Dr. Bell circled the man, peering intently, first at his hands, then his face, and, finally, his gaze fell on a slender leather holster hanging from the patient's belt, flat against his buttock. He returned to his chair and stretched out his legs.

"Mr. MacLure, are you employed as a gravedigger at Greyfriars?"

The man's face contorted and his eyes shifted about the room as if seeking an escape. "No, Doctor. Never been near Greyfriars."

Bell's voice turned sharp. "Unfortunately, the mud on your boots tells a different story—one that is a bit more truthful."

MacLure's face went pale, and, in a moment, the tips of his fingers turned from blushing red to dead white. I thought back to last year when several young people had gone missing. They all were presumed to be dead and all had last been seen walking by Greyfriars Kirkyard. For many months all of Edinburgh was filled with fear of walking at night through that part of town.

"Well, then, Mr. MacLure, if you are not a gravedigger, what is your profession?"

"I got no job right now."

"Eh, but you once were an iceman on the high lochs?"

"Aye." MacLure's eyebrows went up in surprise. "How did you know?"

Bell rose from his chair and took the patient's right hand. "You noted how his fingers underwent a rapid color change. They turned from red to white and are now changing back to blue. This is a sign of Raynaud's disease, named for our French colleague who first observed this phenomenon in 1862. It occurs mainly in women, but also in men who work in the cold or have repetitive injuries to their hands. Damage to the small blood vessels reduces blood flow to the fingers and toes. On warming, an increased flow of blood causes the color changes. Emotional distress, as from telling a lie, also causes the fingers to change color."

I was dumbfounded, when Dr. Bell, quick as a cat, reached around the patient and removed a slender steel spike from the holster at his belt. "This ice pick is used to divide blocks of ice, aye?"

MacLure did not respond.

Bell held the sharp pointed steel pick in front of MacLure's face. "You were acquainted with Professor Corcoran, were you not?"

"Damn you to hell!" The huge man lunged at Bell, who neatly stepped away.

I wanted to help Dr. Bell, but I froze and stood there like a daft galoot.

Fortunately, a couple of the other medical students dove onto the brute, but it was like taking down an oak tree. MacLure did not budge until two more students plunged down the steps and jumped onto him. The four of them wrestled the giant to the floor of the amphitheatre.

"Call the police!" students cried. MacLure struggled violently until Dr. Bell went behind the brute, grabbed his head, and dramatically held the ice pick at the back on his neck, the point pressing into the flesh. "See here, gentlemen. By inclining the head forward, I can easily press the pick through the foramen magnum at the base of the skull, directly into the medulla oblongata and on into the center of the brain. The victim will die instantly, with no more than a barely detectable pin prick on his neck. An autopsy will demonstrate what appears to be a spontaneous cerebral hemorrhage."

During the tense seconds while Bell held the ice pick tight against MacLure's neck, I remembered the horrible moment in Professor Corcoran's anatomy lab last year when I recognized Allison Davies, a fellow student, on his dissecting table.

At first all we saw was her cold, marble-white body, as lovely as the Venus de Milo. Professor Corcoran opened her skull and revealed clots on the surface of her brain. The professor sliced open the brain and found hemorrhaging within the cerebral cortex.

In fact, all of Corcoran's cadavers seemed to have brain hemorrhages. Suspicion fell on Corcoran, but, until this moment, there had been no proof of foul play.

"Doctor Bell, wait. How is this man related to the cadavers in Professor Corcoran's anatomy laboratory?" I had to ask.

"My dear Doyle. Observe, deduce, and connect. I would wager that our Mr. MacLure was formerly in the employ of Corcoran and is 'The Greyfriars Killer!' "

There was a great hubbub of excited conversation. MacLure grunted and tried to escape, but Bell pushed the ice pick a bit deeper into his neck until he drew blood. Could it be true? I had little doubt that Bell, with his powers of observation, had proved that the bodies in Professor Corcoran's laboratory were the victims of the vicious MacLure. No wonder the professor always had perfect bodies for dissection.

Suddenly, with one final burst of energy, MacLure screamed and threw the boys off. He got his hands around Dr. Bell's neck just as a half-dozen police officers burst in and grabbed him. MacLure gave up. The officers dragged the Greyfriars Killer off to prison.

Dr. Bell straightened, cleared his throat, and the smallest hint of a smile etched itself on the side of his mouth. "That is all for today, lads. Thank you very much."

As I packed my books, I could not help but admire Dr. Bell's observational and deductive skills. I was in awe of this brilliant, extraordinary man and knew I needed to document all aspects of my time with him as a clerk.

Just as I was about to file out of the great amphitheatre, a messenger arrived with a letter for the good professor. I followed the messenger as he made his way to Dr. Bell and handed him the stained envelope, which was marked 'URGENT'.

"This is most unsettling. The envelope was postmarked in Chicago on July 11, yet it only just arrived today." He slit open the envelope and scanned the letter.

"Read this, Mr. Doyle," said he.

Dear Dr. Joseph Bell,

As the President of the Board of Trustees of Rush Medical College, I wish to cordially invite you to perform a series of lectures and demonstrations on the antiseptic surgical techniques practised in Edinburgh. These lectures will inaugurate the mid-term which begins on October 12. An honorarium of one thousand pounds sterling will be paid to you upon completion of these lectures and we shall also cover food, travel, and lodging for you and an assistant. I am enclosing steamship and rail tickets for your journey from Glasgow to Chicago.

I also wish to retain your professional services on a personal matter. As you know, I own one of the largest railroad companies in America. I care deeply about my employees, and several young gentlemen who work for me have suddenly collapsed, ceesed breathing, only to then have died within minutes of some enigmatic illness which has defied diagnosis by our best physicians. I pray that you can be of some assistance to me in solving this perplexing mystery.

Yours, very sincerely,

Angus Duncan, Chairman of the Board of Trustees

"Mr. Doyle, what is strange about this letter, aside from the rather lengthy delay in its delivery?"

I re-read the letter. "Um … Eh … Nothing I can see, sir. It appears to be an ordinary invitation."

"Not exactly, lad … Please, note the thickening of the upstroke on the letters 'L' and 'H' in the second paragraph when the author applied firmer pressure to the pen. Also in the second paragraph, the word 'ceased' is misspelt. The author's hand trembled when he signed his name. And why did he use the word 'solving' rather than diagnosing? I deduce that he suspects foul play in the death of his friends and fears for his life."

I examined the letter again. Dr. Bell's keen ability to analyze handwriting had enabled him to detect slight elements which I had missed.

"Angus Duncan was my classmate at the Academy. He was a bit of a scoundrel and the black sheep of his family, but, upon emigrating to America, he made a fortune during the Civil War and is now a respectable railroad baron."

Dr. Bell then studied the steamship tickets. "These tickets are for the *Devonia* that sails from Glasgow on the morning tide to-morrow," he said in his high-pitched voice.

He consulted his gold pocket watch. "And we have missed the last train to Glasgow. Doyle, be quick—there is not a moment to lose. Harry will drive us."

"But, sir. It is more than sixty miles, and, surely, I can't go with—"

"Of course you will accompany me. You are my clerk. If we act post-haste, we can make it in time."

He swept up his leather instrument case and was out of the door onto Lauriston Street. In an instant he spotted Harry, his footman, waiting in a barouche carriage. "Home, Harry, with great alacrity . . . Mr. Doyle, get in. Quick, quick."

It was ludicrous. I had my studies, and we would never make it in time. I glanced at Dr. Bell, ready to object.

He instantly knew my thoughts. "My dear Doyle, quit being an *auld strangy wifie*. The game's afoot and we are about to embark on the greatest adventure of your young life."

"But, my studies—"

"On this trip, I assure you, you will receive an education far beyond what you could get at university."

"Aye, but I can't well afford to just—"

"Aye, ye can. I'll pay you a stipend for your time. I shall give your mother your entire year's clerkship salary in advance. You will finally be free from worry about money."

"How do you know so much about my . . . I have never told you—"

"Observation. And where is your sense of adventure, laddie? At your age you should be ripe for a journey."

He had me there. I had always yearned to go on a grand adventure and try my hand at being like my heroes in the adventure books. How could I refuse such an opportunity?

Our carriage dashed past the castle in a drizzling rain, then on to Princes Street where old ladies were still selling pies to students under the gas lights. Harry whipped up the matched bays and we were off to Dr. Bell's grand residence at 20 Melville Place.

As I sat next to him in silence in the coach, I wondered why this esteemed man of science cared about me. Was he merely looking for a buffoon to mock in America or did he truly see some unrealized potential in me?

Several times I tried to muster up the courage to talk to him. Soon we pulled up to his home and he lurched to the door with his unsteady gait, the result of nerve damage from diphtheria that he had contracted from a young patient.

He was no sooner through his front door when he shouted for his valet. "Willum, pack the Gladstone bag and my steamer trunk. We shall be gone for a month." He thrust a handful of bills into Harry's hand. "Take young Mr. Doyle to his lodgings and give this money to his mother. Be quick!"

I felt like the Prince of Wales as I sat with Dr. Bell's footman in the open carriage while it raced through the yellowish fog of *Auld Reekie*.

"Whoa! Whoa!" Harry yelled ten minutes later, as he stopped the horses in front our squalid rented rooms on Heriot Row.

I flung open the front door. Maw was home, but my Da was probably at the pub getting stinking drunk. "Maw, I am going to America with Dr. Bell," I said. Harry came up, touched his cap, and gave Maw the envelope filled with my clerk's salary for the whole year. Maw and I hugged for a moment. "Don't tell Da about the money."

"I'll save it for your return."

"No, buy a new dress for all the girls, get Innes new shoes, and save the rest for food this winter."

"That's kind of you, Arthur, but what about your studies?"

"Dr. Bell said that I'll learn more in one month in America than I would in two at years in school."

"But, how will you pay—"

"Dr. Bell promised me a stipend on this trip. I shall be back by winter term. I must hurry and pack."

I had only the clothes on my back, but Maw found an extra undershirt and her home-knitted heavy wool stockings, and gave me her bright red wool scarf. I put my meager belongings into a cloth bag along with Macaulay's *History of England*, Cooper's *The Last of The Mohicans*, and a collection of short stories by Edgar Allen Poe. I also packed a blank notebook so I could record my experiences with Dr. Bell. Perhaps, one day, I will have material for stories. Maw also scrounged up my favourite things to eat—a few apples, a pear, a box of sardines, and a packet of butterscotch candies.

I left, but ran back in to give my Maw a big hug. She cried, but I pecked her cheek with a kiss. "I love you, Maw. Thanks," I said.

Harry whipped up the matched bay horses and we were back at Dr. Bell's home in minutes. The doctor was in the library, before an open gun cabinet, loading a stubby British Bull Dog revolver and a handful of .44 calibre cartridges. It was a deadly weapon at short range. "Is that really necessary?" I asked.

"I daresay we may encounter ruffians in Chicago," he said, while carefully hiding the gun in a compartment of his instrument case.

We lay our bags and a wicker basket on the floor of the carriage and covered ourselves with a rug. Harry gave a command and we went at a trot through the streets of Edinburgh. When we reached the macadam roadway, Harry urged the horses to a gallop.

Dr. Bell wore a top hat and a black overcoat about the city, but, now, he was clad in a heavy Inverness cape coat and a deerstalker wool cap with earflaps, raiment usually worn by countrymen. I remembered Dr. Bell made many a cold trip to care for his patients. We were beyond the city, and galloping furiously through open country, when he extinguished his beautifully carved Meerschaum pipe, slouched down, and went fast to sleep. He was obviously accustomed to late night calls to the country.

My thick tweed coat repelled the drizzling rain like a duck's downy feathers, but cold water seeped in around my collar and, soon, I shivered from the wet and cold. I pulled Maw's old scarf tighter, and, after a while, drowsed off.

I was awakened by Dr. Bell's voice. "An extra guinea if you change the horses within five minutes." We had stopped at a livery stable to exchange our exhausted horses for a new team. With straw sticking out of his hair, and rubbing sleep from his eyes, the stable boy brought out new horses. Within five minutes, we were on our way.

Dr. Bell opened the wicker basket and removed a silver flask and a quantity of foodstuffs wrapped in a napkin.

"Mr. Doyle, a sip of this may warm your weary bones."

I waved it off. After seeing what liquor had done to my father over the years I had made a vow never to take a drop of spirits.

"Ah, laddie, a wee dram is good for the body and soul," said he.

He was right. A sip of the malt whisky warmed my stomach. Suddenly, I was ravenous. My last meal had been oatmeal and milk at breakfast, almost a day ago.

"My maw packed a snack," said I.

"Save it for later. My cook packed these viands for our journey."

I started on a chicken leg and then devoured a sandwich. By the time I had finished smoked salmon and rum cake we were nearing the outskirts of Glasgow. It was still many a mile to the steamship docks on the Clyde.

The Tollbooth tower clock struck five as we trotted through Glasgow Cross. Dr. Bell roused from his slumber. "Harry, faster! The ship leaves on the tide."

We were not going to make it. Harry bellowed and cursed at the horses. I prayed that the ship might leave a few minutes late.

At last, we reached the docks as the eastern sky grew lighter. I was barely able to make out the black funnel of our ship amongst the masts and derricks.

"*Devonia*, hold for special passengers. HOLD GODDAMNIT!!!" Harry commanded, with a thunderous shout.

He whipped up the tired horses for the final dash, and we arrived just as the dockhands were releasing the hawsers that held the gangplank.

Dr. Bell gave five guineas to Harry. "You've done wonders to-night. I am deeply grateful. Get yourself a pint, some food and rest," said he.

He would not trust the instrument case to the ship's men, but insisted that I carry the precious load. It was heavy, and I was anxious to get aboard the ship. At the top of the gangplank, I was stopped dead by the sight of a pale and lovely face looking out at the dock.

Sad, tearful green eyes. Flaming red hair hanging in ringlets about her pale, delicate features. A lovely, ethereal angel.

The most beautiful creature I had ever seen was standing before me.

And then, she waved.

My heart raced.

Of all the men on the ship, she chose to wave at me!

I smiled, and, as I was about to wave back, I sadly realized that she was waving at a lad of no more than twelve years who happened to be standing on the dock right behind me.

"Miss Yates, stop that mewling. Jimmy needs you this instant," a sharp, gruff voice suddenly intoned.

She turned and disappeared. What was I thinking? My medical studies came first. I had no time for women.

My euphoria vanished into the mist as I heard a familiar voice. "Doyle, there is no time to dawdle. Hurry along and take my instrument case to our cabin."

I grabbed the bags and grimaced. Was I his lackey? I wanted to throttle Dr. Bell.

26 September, 1878

By the time Dr. Bell and I settled in our cramped quarters my wet clothing left puddles of water on our stateroom floor. I sneezed and had a fit of shivering as I carefully stowed the instrument case beneath Dr. Bell's bunk and then collapsed onto my own.

I was cold, wet, and tired, yet, for the first time in a year, I was free from the Edinburgh Infirmary and the pressures of university. I was grateful for the change. For a few days, I would be a man of leisure.

The purser, a muscular black man, brought the Gladstone bag, trunk, and my cloth bag.

With a flourish, he unpacked the trunk and arranged Dr. Bell's clothing in our closet. He then removed my shirt and the extra stockings from my bag and stacked my books on a small shelf. He did all of this with a genuine smile on his face. When he was finished, he turned to me with a quizzical look. "Is this all, sir?" he asked.

"Aye, that's it. What is your name?" I inquired.

"My name is Bub, once a slave, but a freeman now. Sirs, the first gong will announce breakfast after the ship is underway." Dr. Bell gave him a shilling while I struggled out of my wet coat.

"Good heavens, Mr. Doyle, have you no dry clothing?"

"Only a shirt and a pair of stockings, sir."

"We are first-class passengers. You can't go about looking like a pauper, laddie."

But, I am a pauper, and a dirt poor one at that, but no laddie. I am a man of almost twenty-years! Why did Bell always ride me so hard? "Try these," he said, just as I was about to make a tart response. He took a dark green wool jacket and grey trousers from the closet.

We were of about the same height, both over six feet tall, but, from playing rugger and boxing, I had more muscle. The coat was tight across the shoulders, but, left unbuttoned, the fit was not too bad and the trousers were perfect.

I felt like a true gentleman, rather than a poor student, and was instantly ashamed of myself. The professor had a streak of humanity after all. Warmth returned. "Thank you, sir," I managed to say, after a fit of sneezing.

The ship's engine rumbled, and a great blast from its horn announced the *Devonia*'s progress down the Clyde. A gong sounded with a sharp *clang*. "That is for breakfast," I said.

"I am not the least hungry." Dr. Bell laid out writing material, his books and papers on the small desk under our porthole and set to work on revising his manual of surgery.

The first-class saloon in the middle section of the ship was as fine as any gentleman's club. There were tables for six. Wood paneling and portraits of great ships lined the walls. Off-duty ship officers were at one table, but it was early and there were only a few other diners.

I had no sooner selected a table where I could be alone with my whirling thoughts about Dr. Bell and that red-haired girl when a white-coated waiter poured a cup of strong tea from a silver pot and left a tray of toast and marmalade.

This was followed by rashers of bacon, fried and boiled eggs, potatoes, a mutton chop, and kippered herrings. I felt obliged to eat everything, and, out of a sense of duty and moral obligation, I also forced down an apple tart, a pear tart, and another cup of tea.

The ship was vibrating as we steamed with the tide down the River Clyde. The wind that blew across the deck was invigorating, but, after the long night and hearty meal, I could not fight off drooping eyelids and a feeling of lassitude.

I journeyed back to our cabin. Dr. Bell was inside, reading and chewing on a gangly ginger root. I climbed into the upper bunk.

27 September, 1878

I slept until well past noon yesterday, and awoke to a peculiarly unpleasant sensation in the pit of my stomach. Dr. Bell was still at the small desk, his legs stretched out, while he read from a textbook of surgery and wrote a few lines on a sheet of foolscap. The entire room was rolling, and even the papers and ink pot on the desk slid from one side to the other with the ship's motion.

"Tsk, tsk, young Doyle. You slept away the best part of the day. We are well out in the Firth of Clyde and shall soon round the Mull of Kintyre to the North Channel."

I hardly heard his words when I was overcome with the two terrible sensations of whirling about and nausea. I tried swallowing back the copious amounts of spit and acid, but they kept coming back up. I made it to the side of the ship just in time.

My prodigious breakfast splashed into the sea. For the rest of the day and night I gagged and heaved into a bucket provided by the gentle purser, Bub.

"Ah, my boy, you should know ginger root is a capital remedy for *mal de mer*, but it is only effective as a preventative, not as a cure," said Dr. Bell.

By this afternoon, we were well out in the Atlantic Ocean and the ship was steadier. I held down a spot of tea and set out on unsteady feet for a walk. Passengers were lounging on deck chairs covered by heavy blankets, but there was no sign of the red-haired girl.

I then ventured onto the more crowded second-class deck and down a series of ladders to steerage, where hundreds of poor emigrants slept in their clothing on hard tiers of shelves. The noise and stink of vomit and unwashed bodies was unbearable. *This is where I really belong*, I thought, and, for a moment, I was ready to abandon my first-class cabin.

There was no sign of that wonderful and mysterious red-haired girl.

Back on the open deck, I filled my lungs with a bit of fresh air and felt better. I even thought about food once again. Halfway down the port side, just aft of the funnel, I came across a lanky, pale fellow with long brown hair and a wispy mustache wearing a stained velvet coat. He was resting on a nest of coiled rope and canvas, scribbling in a notebook, with his face to the warm sun. It took me a moment to recognize him—he was an old mate whom had been several years ahead of me at Edinburgh University.

"Stevenson, old fellow, what are you doing here?"

"Arthur, I could say the same to you, you old sod." Robert Louis Stevenson swept away a lock of dark hair that hung over his eyes.

"You first, and then I'll tell my tale."

"I'm off to California to meet the woman I love. What about you?"

"I'm with Dr. Joseph Bell, a faculty member at Edinburgh. I am his outpatient clerk, although, sometimes, I feel more like his valet than a medical assistant. The doctor is to give lectures in America."

"Ah, yes. I remember Bell is a great surgeon, second only to Lister himself. And Lister, you know, helped my dear friend, William Ernest Henley, the poet. London doctors had amputated one of his legs for tuberculosis of the bone and wanted to take his other leg as well. Lister kept poor Henley in bed and saved his one leg with surgery and carbolic dressings. Your field is dreadfully gory, Arthur."

Stevenson's face turned unusually pale, and he was wracked with a deep cough. He got up from his nest and barely made it to the railing to spit out a gob of yellow mucous. The poor man was little more than skin and bone and appeared to be deathly ill. "I prefer the gilded fantasy of fiction," said he.

"I remember seeing you with Henley on the surgical wards. Weren't you studying law then?" I asked.

"Engineering first, and then the law, aye. All the while, though, I felt as if I was lost upon the seven seas. A man without a calling . . . But, you, my dear friend, don't seem to have that problem. Your true love is the medical arts, aye?"

"Well, medical school has been a long, weary grind of botany, chemistry, anatomy, physiology, and subjects that seem to have little bearing upon the art of curing."

"Ah yes, the dull, mind-numbing grind of studies . . . Why do you think I am here and not back there?"

"In all honesty, I yearn for adventure and dream of sitting at my desk and penning famous tales like Poe, but that will never happen. I come from a humble background and shall practise medicine so that I will always have two pence to pay the taxman."

"Quite the pragmatic choice, but . . . I prefer your dream life . . . To be able to support oneself only through the might of the pen. That would be a dream come true."

I gestured to the men swarming up the mast, setting the sails to catch the following breeze. "Well then, mate, why don't you write of this adventure? Spice it up a bit with some buried treasure and pirates and I'll wager you might garner the interest of a London publishing house," said I.

"I could not. I haven't the skills nor imagination."

"Then, like Shakespeare himself, base your characters on real figures, such as Henley."

He coughed. "What do you mean?"

"Henley, with his wooden leg, could serve as the model for a murderous pirate. Can't you just hear the thump of his stump on a tavern floor or the deck of a sailing ship?"

"I would not want to offend poor Henley, especially after he's been through so much."

"You need not worry if you alter his character a bit. Make up a fitting moniker. Let us see . . . With only one leg, you might call him something like 'Short John' and give him a murderous craving for silver coin."

"Hmmm . . . That is a thought worth considering. I often carry pencil and paper with the hope of someday capturing a good yarn." Poor Stevenson had another fit of coughing.

"And you might also consider consulting with Dr. Bell about your lungs."

"You sawbones are all alike. The doctors in France recommended a year at bed rest and the Germans prescribed hot baths. It is all tomfoolery. For me, the prescription's simple—travel, a warm woman, and a hot climate. I do not intend to waste away in bed, but will live as I like and shall die with my boots on."

"I see. And speaking of women, Robert, have you spied a lovely lass with wild red hair on the ship?"

"Ah yes, Arthur. I see that working with Dr. Bell has also helped your powers of observation."

"Do you know her, by chance?"

"I do."

"So tell, my friend . . . Tell all."

"I would, but I do apologize. I have a pressing engagement . . ." He started to get up. I grabbed him by the forearm and implored him with a stare and my firm grip. "I give in . . . Her name is Rebecca. Rebecca Yates. She is a nurse to the spoiled brat son of a Presbyterian minister."

"By the name of?"

"James Balfour. The insufferable man is a distant cousin of my mother and recently dismissed from a church in Aberdeen. "

"I see . . . Hmmm . . ."

"Oh, Arthur, do join me to-morrow night for the evening's entertainment in the companionway between steerage three and four."

"I can't make it. I must be sure to study my medical texts and keep my diary up to date."

"Dear, misguided Arthur, put your beloved books aside and live. It should be quite a frolic. I promise such a bevy of busty lassies. You'll soon forget red-haired Rebecca."

"We shall see." I smiled and bid Robert farewell.

28 September, 1878

After the evening meal I scribbled down the day's events, read for a few hours, but needed a break, so I met Stevenson in his second-class cabin just forward of the companionway. His room was little more than an open space in the deckhouse, lit by a wildly swinging lantern. Through a side door there were glimpses of the night sea. Couples were already whirling about, dancing to the music of a fiddle.

Down below on the first landing, near coils of rope and a huge capstan, a half-dozen Irish girls danced a lively jig. Stevenson was right. Several of them caught my attention, but their green eyes never rested on me. They were more interested in the sailors. After a few pints of beer I was eager for a dance or a kiss, but those thoughts were unworthy of Rebecca. And, besides, the lassies had picked out their sailors.

The evening wore on, and the company grew to at least thirty or forty people, including a few from the first-class cabins. The fiddler played a bastard doggerel from the music halls accompanied by onlookers keeping time by beating tin pans with spoons.

As the evening came to a close, a particularly comely Irish girl, with painted lips and a saucy smile, climbed on the capstan and danced to a rousing jig. She kicked up her legs and, at the end, turned her back on the audience, flung up her skirt, and aimed her backside at the audience. There was wild applause and shouts of "More! More!" but, at that very moment, the bosun arrived. "All turn in!" he bellowed.

I bid Stevenson a bleary "Good night," and staggered back to my cabin.

29 September, 1878

After only a few hours of sleep, during the deep dark of night, I was awakened by beating on our door. Dr. Bell, in his nightclothes, opened the door to reveal the ship's Captain and two armed sailors.

"Dr. Bell, sir, sorry to trouble you at this ungodly hour. Would you be so kinds as to see a gravely ill passenger?" the Captain asked.

Dr. Bell threw his heavy Inverness cape coat over his night clothing, while I quickly donned my tweed coat. The wind had come up again, and, as we made our way to the passenger's cabin, we were assaulted by sea spray. Clouds closed in on the ship's masts making the night even gloomier.

The victim was the same Irish girl who had danced so madly on the capstan only a few hours ago. The swinging lanterns provided only a fitful light, but one of the sailors produced a bullseye lamp to illuminate her body. The poor girl's swollen, black tongue protruded between her lips, and her eyes bulged as if in mortal fear. There was no pulse or heartbeat, but the body was still warm.

"She is well beyond my care," Dr. Bell said.

"I thought as much. Can you determine the cause of death?" asked the Captain.

The skin on her neck was red, badly abraded, and her throat was almost cut through just beneath her jaw.

"Death was certainly due to strangulation. Note the twist marks. I should think she was attacked from behind. The murderer used a twisted chain or heavy cord about an eighth of an inch in diameter," Dr. Bell said.

There was another strange finding. Her bodice was open, and written with the girls own lip paint across her breasts was the word "Tzabel." Neither of us, for all our study of Latin, Greek, and French, knew the word. It was a mystery.

"Captain, I suggest that you maintain absolute secrecy about the mode of death and this word," Dr. Bell said.

His head was sunk in thought while I made ready for bed. "It is unlikely that an ignorant sailor committed this crime. I believe the murder was the work of an educated man," said he.

4 October, 1878

Nothing eventful has occurred over the past few days, thus, I have not written any new entries here. Today, fresh rumors are flying about the ship. Many passengers are certain that a crewman committed the fiendish murder. Women will not walk about the decks alone, and even the men have taken to carrying personal weapons.

This morning, I paid a courtesy visit to the sick bay in the hope of furthering my education in regards to the practise of medicine at sea. The ship's doctor was a trembling American with a purple nose and broken veins in his cheeks. One glance at his untidy desk and nearly empty medicine cabinet told the story of a man long gone to drink. As I looked at him and his quarters, I tried not to think of my own Da.

The ship's doctor gave heroic doses of mercury to the crew for their chronic venereal disease and prescribed opium in alcohol for the passengers so that they might sleep through the voyage.

Desperate for better care, several passengers requested a consultation with Dr. Bell. These culminated in Bub bringing a request for Dr. Bell to see a sick child. My heart quickened when I saw that the note was signed by none other than a Mrs. James Balfour.

I followed the good doctor, carrying his black medicine bag, hoping to meet or at least see Miss Rebecca

Yates. When Miss Yates, herself, opened the door, I was overcome, turned red in the face, and lost the power of speech.

Dr. Bell bowed and introduced himself to the Reverend Balfour and to his wife. I stood, blushing, holding the black bag. "My capable assistant, Mr. Arthur Conan Doyle," said he.

The minister was a mild-mannered, meek man of about forty who stood aside while his wife wiped tears from her eyes and showed us to the bedside of their five-year-old son. Her deeply lined face was creased with worry and she wrung her hands. "Oh Doctor, thank you for coming. Poor Jimmy hasn't had a moment's rest. I fear it is typhoid."

I would never have noticed, but Dr. Bell's eyes were immediately drawn to the heavy twisted gold watch chain that crossed the minister's chest from one vest pocket to another.

"Has anyone in the family been ill? Reverend Balfour, do you feel well?" Dr. Bell asked.

"I was a trifle indisposed last night, but am quite well this morning."

"Just to be sure, I should check your pulse. May I use your watch?"

"Certainly."

The Reverend Balfour snapped open his heavy gold watch and passed the instrument with its peculiar chain to Dr.

Bell, who ostentatiously held the man's wrist while counting his pulse. I was puzzled when Dr. Bell ran a fingernail over the length of the gold chain. Had he, with his famous powers of observation, noted a detail that I had missed?

"Your pulse is quite normal. May I ask a question?"

"Of course," the minister said.

"Are you acquainted with the word Tzabel? T-z-a-b-e-l?"

"That is old Hebrew for Jezebel, an evil woman, the wife of Ahab, in First and Second Kings." There was no trace of nervousness or anxiety in his voice. Reverend Balfour could have been preaching a sermon.

Suddenly, a look of comprehension passed over Dr. Bell's face. Had he deduced who the killer was?

Jimmy made a most piteous cry, demanding attention. Dr. Bell did not speak, but sat by the boy, chin on his hand, and turned his penetrating gaze to the lad. Without a word, he placed his hand on the boy's abdomen. Jimmy clenched his eyes and writhed in pain.

I was certain the poor child was suffering from the last stages of peritonitis when Jimmy half opened one eye to peer about the room. Then, when he thought no one was looking, a brief smile came over his face as if he were having a grand old time being the center of attention.

Dr. Bell probed his abdomen for an enlarged liver or spleen, then counted the pulse. "Young man, please open your mouth and stick out your tongue."

"What did he eat last evening?"

"He cleaned his plate of beef, potatoes, gravy, bread, milk, and a bit of pie. We all had the same meal, but it couldn't have been the food," his mother said.

"When did he have the raspberry jam and chocolate?" Bell asked.

"We never allow him to have sweets."

Dr. Bell wiped his finger across the edge of the lad's mouth and displayed a sticky red smear with tell-tale raspberry seeds. Next, he held up the lad's right hand. "If you will, Mrs. Balfour, please sample this brown substance on his right index finger. It is chocolate, a Dutch chocolate if I am not mistaken."

I had peered over his shoulder and had seen none of these clues. Again, I felt like an oaf, unfit to practise medicine.

"Your son's greedy, that's all. He's a glutton. Give him a dose of castor oil and no food for the rest of the day," said Dr. Bell, with an uncharacteristically harsh tone. He was usually so gentle with children.

The mild-mannered Reverend Balfour was suddenly transformed. His once-placid face became contorted into a dark rictus of hatred. His lips pulled back, exposing yellowing teeth, and his eyes sunk into slits buried within horrid wrinkles. In an instant he had become a beast—an aged, horrid beast with outstretched, claw-like fingers.

Balfour took up a sewing case and swung it with all his might at Dr. Bell's head. "Damned bloody bastard! No one calls my son a glutton."

Dr. Bell ducked, and the sewing case smashed against the wall of the cabin, where it splintered—sending needles and thread flying about the room. The Reverend Balfour swayed as if he would fall, but, then, lurched across the small room towards Rebecca. "It was you, witch! You gave him the chocolate!" His scream ended with a hideous choking and gurgling in his throat.

I blocked him before he reached the poor girl, who had collapsed into a heap against the wall. Then, we watched in horror as the minister's right arm jerked with uncontrollable spasms and his right leg collapsed.

He fell to the floor with his legs jerking convulsively. Powerful neck muscles, contracting like iron bars, pulled his head backwards until I thought his neck would dislocate. He lapsed into unconsciousness.

As his mouth clenched tightly and his breathing became labored, Dr. Bell urged, "Doyle, open his mouth. Don't let his tongue fall back."

What was I supposed to do? I hesitated and trembled when Rebecca handed me a spoon. I stood there, doing nothing, until she grabbed the spoon, jammed it through the clenched teeth, and pried open the man's mouth. I pulled myself together and grasped his slobbery tongue. His breathing became less labored.

"A light. I need a light, please." Dr. Bell said.

Rebecca lit a candle, which the doctor held before the sick man's eyes. The pupil of his right eye contracted normally in response to the light, but there was no reaction in the left eye. "The fact that his left pupil doesn't contract in the light doesn't bode well. Has he had these spells in the past or complained of headaches?"

Mrs. Balfour sobbed uncontrollably and could not answer. "He has suffered unbearable headaches for the past year and has had similar, though milder, spells," said Rebecca. "Dr. Balfour was dismissed from his church when he had an attack during a service and smashed the altar," she barely whispered.

The epileptic fit had passed, but the Reverend Balfour was in a deep coma. His tongue no longer fell back in his throat, but he struggled to breathe, with harsh, labored gasps. Dr. Bell again knelt by the man and carefully probed the left side of his head. "Mr. Doyle, feel this."

There was the slightest elevation and irregularity of the scalp above and behind his left eye forward of the ear. "What is it, sir?" I asked.

"Elementary," said Dr. Bell. "This is a case of Jacksonian epilepsy, caused by a tumor pressing on his brain. I fear he is hemorrhaging from the tumor. We must elevate the bone to relieve the pressure on the brain and, if possible, remove the tumor."

Dr. Bell rose to his height. "We must operate immediately. Have the sick bay scrubbed with carbolic until it is sparkling clean. We will need freshly laundered, boiled linen." Under the circumstances, I could not understand how he was so calm and determined.

"But, sir, trephining the skull is dangerous, even in a hospital."

"Believe, me this is for the best," said he.

Rebecca commandeered two housekeepers to scrub the sick bay walls and floor with strong soap. I washed the operating table and a desk for the instruments with dilute carbolic acid.

Dr. Bell ordered the Captain to slow the ship and put her on a stable course.

"Damn, we will be late to New York!" The angry red-faced Captain spluttered.

"It is the law of the sea. You must obey a doctor when there is a medical emergency," Dr. Bell said.

Bub and another purser carried the unconscious man to the newly scrubbed sick bay and, as gently as any nurse, placed him on the table with the left side of his head uppermost. A moment later, Dr. Bell walked in and his face fell. The small room was only illuminated by a tiny porthole. "This'll never do. There's too little light for a delicate operation."

Stevenson, sensing a possible story, had slipped into the sick bay. "Dr. Bell, if you will, I have an idea."

"And who, exactly, are you, lad?"

"Robert Louis Stevenson, at your service. I have a bit of experience with lighting and would like to try something if you'll allow me . . . Doyle, hand me those oil lanterns and that looking glass."

Dr. Bell grew interested. "Hmm . . . Aye, but Stevenson, can you create a bright light?"

"We shall see," Stevenson said as he placed four lanterns on a shelf above the operating table. With a calculating eye, he placed the mirror in front of the lanterns, which he angled down to concentrate light at the patient's head.

"Stevenson, where did you learn that ingenious trick?" I asked.

"I'm from a family of lighthouse engineers and I even gave a paper on mirrors and light to the Royal Society." He turned up the flames, bathing the patient's head in light as if he was outdoors on a sunny day. Amazing!

Bell ran his hands through the bright light. "Quite ingenious."

I set out the scalpels, chisels, trephine, forceps, needles, and stitches, all freshly soaked in carbolic, on a clean white sheet. We then rolled up our sleeves and scrubbed our hands with a mild carbolic solution. Our patient remained in a deep coma, but he breathed better and his pulse was strong.

"Lassie, can you thread needles?" Dr. Bell asked.

"I have threaded needles since I was five years old," Miss Rebecca Yates replied.

"Good. Thread the needles with silk and keep the instruments in good order," he replied.

Bub, clearly a man of many talents, had shaved and washed the minister's head. It shone in the bright light.

Bell turned to Bub. "Hold his head, like so, with the left side uppermost. It must remain steady. Mr. Doyle, you must be my assistant. If he awakens during the operation, you may have to give him a few drops of chloroform."

I began to panic and could not for the life of me remember the location of the temporal lobe. But, fortunately, Dr. Bell knew exactly what he was doing.

He studied the head as if it were a laboratory specimen. After a moment, he took up a scalpel, and, gently, with its tip, marked the line of incision on the scalp. It was curved above and just forward of an imaginary line drawn between the eye and the ear. "Doyle, here is the line of incision. Press with all your might down on the scalp, please."

This was a job usually reserved for senior surgical house officers. I had never assisted at an operation and felt bile rising in my throat. My right hand commenced to tremble when blood trickled from the scratch.

"Doyle, there is no time to dilly dally. Buck up, lad. Press on the scalp."

Well, I thought, I will use my muscle. After years of playing rugby I was strong. I pressed as hard as possible. There was hardly any bleeding. From the semi-circular scalp incision, he stitched an artery and laid back the scalp to expose an irregular area of bone.

The trephine was little more than a carpenter's brace connected to a round bit designed to bore through bone. When he had made three openings down to the membranes surrounding the brain, he connected the holes with a hammer and chisel.

His only words were, "Bub, if you please, hold the head as still as possible."

Though just a beginning student, I could identify the hard grey tumor that bulged up from the membranes covering the brain. Bell cut around the tumor until the gyri and sulci of the temporal lobe of the brain came into view.

I was completely carried away by seeing a functioning human brain inside a living man's skull. Dr. Bell jolted me out of my reverie. "Please Doyle, help. I can't see to do my work unless you mop away the blood."

With fifteen minutes of concentrated work using forceps and knife, he removed the plum-sized tumor and dropped it into a metal tray.

Dr. Bell used firm pressure and a few stitches to stop blood that trickled from open veins on the surface of the brain. Every time he held out his hand for more stitches, Miss Yates had the needle threaded and ready.

He replaced the bone, sutured the scalp, and applied the carbolic dressings. It was over. I had concentrated so hard on the operation, I forgot my distress, and although my legs trembled, I had passed a milestone in my medical career.

Miss Yates took her leave to care for Mrs. Balfour and Jimmy, and Dr. Bell sent word to the Captain that all was well. Soon, we were steaming at top speed on our original course.

Dr. Bell insisted that our patient remain on the sick bay table until he awoke from his coma. He watched over the unconscious man with brooding eyes. It was near midnight when Stevenson strolled in with a flask of French brandy. He listened to my worried query.

"Dr. Bell, will you notify the Captain about your suspicions of Reverend Balfour? He is surely the murderer."

He gave me a queer look. "The murderer is gone and departed. Reverend Balfour is an innocent man," said Dr. Bell, just as he left for our cabin.

"What does he mean?" I asked Stevenson.

"Dr. Bell must believe it is as if the Reverend Balfour is two people in one or that he has two personalities. The real Balfour is an innocent man. When Dr. Bell removed the tumor, he took away the religious maniac who killed the girl," Stevenson replied. "I would argue that he should not be held liable for the actions of his second, evil self."

Stevenson took a generous pull from the flask. "You know, it might be worth a story," he said, rather idly.

The Reverend Balfour moved an arm, and his eyes fluttered. I checked the pupils of his eyes. They were equal, and he breathed easier.

"You know better than me. If a small tumor can cause a mild-mannered man to become a murdering maniac, could a potion, some sort of witch's brew, do the same?" Stevenson asked.

I thought of my experience at the Hospital for Incurables. "Aye, the brain can react to disease, drugs, or injury in mysterious ways. If you someday return to Edinburgh, look up Dr. Jekyll in the chemistry department. He would certainly be able to provide more information."

Stevenson furiously scribbled in his notebook and offered the bottle. I had to keep my wits about me and refused. "Tell me more about Miss Yates."

He laughed. "You poor, poor sod. You're smitten. Her parents died last year from typhoid fever, leaving her and a young brother in deplorable circumstances. She is distantly related to the Balfours, so the minister took them in. The girl was supposed to be a nurse to the lad, but the wife makes her work like a scullery maid. When he became ill and left the church in Aberdeen, he found a position as a missionary to a tribe of Indians in the far west. He sent the lad to a foundling home and kept the girl to look after his son. I pity the poor heathens who must listen to his dogmatic rants."

I mulled over this tragic story until our patient stirred. He again moved his right arm, and both his eyes flickered for a moment. He uttered a long sigh and grasped my hand. There were more signs of slight, but encouraging, improvement as a new day dawned.

As I sat with him, I was having visions of sweeping Rebecca off her feet and taking her back to Scotland when, suddenly, she entered the sick bay holding a tray with a pot of tea and plate of eggs and bacon. She glanced at Stevenson, but rewarded me with a lovely sunny smile. "Arthur, I have been thinking of you. Poor man, are you famished and exhausted?" she asked.

Her hair was swept back and tied in a severe bun. She wore a drab grey gown, but, to my eyes, she was a vision of loveliness. Without another word, she poured tea and handed me the plate. "Enjoy the food. I must go back to Jimmy now."

She was gone before I could thank her, but, for the next few minutes, her words "I've been thinking of you" danced in my mind.

Then, a sad thought struck home. We were destined to never be together. We were both penniless. I had another year of school and more years before I could support a wife, much less her young brother.

A moment later, Bub entered and told me that Dr. Bell had paid him to look after the Reverend Balfour and I was free to go.

5 October, 1878

After an exhausted sleep I awoke to Stevenson's knock. We strolled a bit and took our usual place in the sun behind the ship's funnel. We had been chatting for a good hour or two when we heard a low moan that could have been wind sighing through the rigging or even a sea bird. Yet there was an immediacy to it that caught our ears.

When the moan became a scream, we leaped to our feet and followed the sound to behind a small deckhouse that served as a sail locker. It was there that we saw a huge sailor attempting to force Rebecca into the locker.

He had one hand to her throat and the other was ripping the front of her gown. We both leapt forward to rescue her. Stevenson reached the man first, but was batted away as if he were a common housefly.

I moved into the fray, but the big sailor loosened his grip on Rebecca and slammed his fist into my mid-section. The blow forced me to my knees, but afforded me a moment to watch the man.

His face was red with lust and rum. His nose was twisted from some long-lost battle. There was a gold hoop ring in one ear and a sheath knife at his belt. A green tattooed sea serpent twisted up one bare arm.

I regained my feet and jumped up as he aimed another blow. I had flailed away with boxing gloves at other students at the university, but this was not a gentlemen's match.

I narrowly avoided his punch, but, as he cocked back his arm for a killing blow, I remembered something I had learned from dissecting an arm in anatomy class: The ulnar nerve behind the elbow is extremely sensitive. With all my might, I aimed my clenched fist at his elbow, where I landed a terrific blow one inch above the medial epicondyle. He must have felt a horrible lightening-like pain because he roared and threw Rebecca in a heap on the deck.

Even though his right arm now hung uselessly at his side, he charged with his head down and reached for my neck with his good left hand.

I stepped to my right and barely avoided being pushed into the ocean. He had his knife half out of its sheath now, and if it had not been for his drunkenness, I would have surely been run through and killed on the spot. Instead, his knife sliced through the air a few inches from my ear.

I swung at his face, but he ducked, and my blow hit his shoulder. I heard the *snap* as his collarbone broke. Before either one of us could get in another blow, the third officer and three sailors subdued the brute.

I felt more than a twinge of jealousy when Stevenson got to Rebecca and whispered consoling phrases into her ear. He even covered her bare bosom with his seedy velvet coat.

Stevenson was a ladies man, and I feared that he might try to take advantage of her distress.

I dashed over and wrapped my tweed coat around her shoulders. Instantly she stepped away from Stevenson and threw her arms around my neck, sobbing convulsively.

I held her close. She moved her head onto my shoulder. We clung together until her sobbing stopped. Holding her was such bliss, such pure sweetness.

"Oh Arthur, you were magnificent. I wish we could spend more time together, but I must get back and help the Balfours."

As we walked to the Balfour's cabin I asked about her life. She still clung tightly to my arm. "When my parents died, I vowed to earn money so I might study medicine in Edinburgh." She said this wistfully as if it were merely a dream.

"Oh, Rebecca, that is possible. The university allows women to study. Some professors don't believe women have the constitution to dissect a cadaver, but Dr. Bell is offering special anatomy classes to a few women. He believes women can be good doctors."

I did my best to comfort her, but she was still trembling when we arrived at the Balfour's cabin. Without another word, she again wiped her eyes, sighed deeply, and then entered the small second-class quarters. Immediately, I heard Mrs. Balfour accuse poor Rebecca of inviting the sailor's advances. "You have dishonoured God and will never know the Lord Jesus!" I turned away with a heavy heart.

6 October, 1878

I attempted to pay Rebecca another visit today, but to no avail. Dr. Bell had sent the minister back to his room, so she nursed him day and night and suffered from the demanding brat, Jimmy, and his angry mother. I spent my time reading medical texts and writing last night's diary entry.

Today, after ten long days at sea, we ended our voyage. We docked at the Battery on the southernmost end of Manhattan Island. Stevenson was the first off the ship, hurrying to take a train across the continent. As he disappeared into the crowd I wondered if I would ever see him again.

As we were packing Bub brought a note from Rebecca. "Please, come to me, immediately, at the place where you usually meet Mr. Stevenson," it read.

She was leaning over the rail, staring at the water and the distant buildings. Worried that she might be about to leap overboard, I ran and took her hand.

"I thought I might never see you again," I said.

"I wanted to thank you for saving me from that brute before we parted forever."

"Forever? Is that Indian reservation so far that we shall never see one another again?"

"Arthur, please." She bent closer and touched my lips with her index finger. As I tried to kiss it, she pulled it away. "You must never tell a soul what I am about to tell you."

"I promise."

"The minister is not going to the Indians. That is just a story to fool people. Just before he became ill he met an American who was traveling in Scotland. This man invited him to preach down South."

"Why would he invite a Scot to preach in America?"

At first, she did not say anything. For a long moment, we watched gulls making great swooping dives in the ship's wake to find tidbits of garbage in the salty water.

"I don't know all the details, but I have a sense that it has to do with a pro-slavery secret society. You see, the Reverend Balfour always preached that the Bible says Negro people are God's disobedient children, the cursed children of Ham, and therefore destined to be slaves to white men."

"But, that is ridiculous. I have read the Bible and I don't see how anyone could reach that conclusion."

"I don't know, but it all scares me. And he mentioned something about us meeting him in a big city on a big river in the middle of America."

"Wherever you end up, Miss Yates, please write and tell me."

"I shall, Mr. Doyle. Where will you be?"

"You can always address the letter to me care of the Rush Medical College."

For a moment I held her close and felt her heart fluttering like a small bird. She pulled away, and, without another word, ran off to the Balfour's stateroom.

Suddenly, I felt empty, forlorn, as if my life had come to a crashing halt. A minute earlier, the world had felt so warm and welcoming and full of promise. Now, it was a lonely, cruel place.

"Doyle, my lad, come. We have work to do." Dr. Bell called and insisted that I join him in visiting our patient. I was red-faced and clumsy in front of Rebecca, but managed to assist with the dressings. "Doyle, take care. Mind the antisepsis," said Dr. Bell. Reverend Balfour had no fever and Dr. Bell found no sign of inflammation in the wound. Our patient could speak, and, although weak, he had full use of his extremities. We learned that the family was to stay with the Reverend Henry Ward Beecher in Brooklyn prior to their trip to the Southland.

Dr. Bell insisted that once the Reverend Balfour settled down in America he seek the services of a former Edinburgh physician to mind the antiseptic dressings. Balfour promised and we exited his stateroom.

I took one last longing look at Rebecca. There were tears in her eyes.

Back in our tiny cabin, Bub was folding and packing Dr. Bell's clothing. "Mr. Doyle, I want to ask a question," said he.

"Why of course, Bub."

"Sir, I can read and write and I've studied lots of medical books. I wanna be a doctor for my people. Can I go with you and Dr. Bell to Chicago as your personal valet? I can sure take care of your things, run errands, and keep your boots shined. And maybe you and the doctor put in a good word for me. Maybe you can help me get into Rush Medical School in Chicago."

I had never known a man of color. The occasional black man in Edinburgh seemed out of place and often menacing, but Bub was different. I liked him, and it would be good to have someone who knew the customs of America with us. I took the matter up with Dr. Bell.

Dr. Bell liked the idea, and we quickly struck a bargain. Bub became our valet and all-purpose assistant for his board, room, and ten dollars a week. I promised to teach him Latin medical terms and some anatomy.

"We can't keep calling you 'Bub.' What name was given to you at birth?" Dr. Bell queried.

"I once had the name of my master, but I ain't used it since I escaped and went up North. I'm scared of using that name because that man is liable to snatch me back."

"But, that's illegal since Mr. Lincoln signed the emancipation proclamation."

"Don't matter. My old master's a ghost and the law don't apply to spirits. He claimed all his slaves are his property forever, no matter what paper Mr. Lincoln signed."

"No one is going to take you back to slavery . . . Out with it . . . You must have a name."

"Rufus 'Bubba' Freeman is what I like being called now."

"I understand. But, before you got that name, what were you called?"

"Well . . ." He looked around nervously. "They used to call me Rufus Bedford Forrest."

"As in General Nathan Bedford Forrest?"

"Yes, sir."

I made a thrust with an imaginary sword. "The dispatches to the London papers carried stories about his exploits. He killed many a Union soldier with pistol and sword."

"The papers reported his death about two years ago, so you need not worry about him," said Dr. Bell.

We all shook hands. Down on the dock Rufus hailed a hansom cab, packed our things, and off we went to a bank to exchange our pounds and shillings for dollars. Then, to my great surprise, Dr. Bell ordered the cab to the nearest haberdasher to outfit me with a suit of clothes and new shoes.

I preened before the mirror in my new grey suit with a fine white shirt and a cravat. Just as my head was filling with thoughts of my splendor, I heard my mother's voice echoing in the back of my mind, and my spirits fell. "Arthur, you must never live above your station. Remember who you are."

Was Dr. Bell decking me in fine garments to show me off to his rich American friends as a sort of well-dressed, trained monkey?

7 October, 1878

I felt much better this morning after having eaten a big porterhouse steak, oysters, turtle soup, and ale in the hotel dining room last night.

Early this morning, Rufus proved his worth by guiding us through this strange, crowded, bustling city to the station just in time to catch the train that would take us across half a continent.

Our compartment had couches that the porter folded down at night and made up with fresh linen for sleeping. Rufus stowed our bags, but, as usual, I was in charge of the instrument case.

Dr. Bell settled in our compartment and returned to writing *A Manual of Surgery* and smoking his meerschaum pipe. Meanwhile, I explored the observation car, read my books, and searched the passing landscape in vain for some sign of Cooper's Mohicans or at least a Mohawk squaw.

I am sad to report that I did not seen a single red man between New York City and Chicago. I had to be satisfied with the villages, cities, large fields of corn and wheat, and great herds of cattle that we whirled past. It was all so different from our wee country in the north of Britain. The dining car was as elaborate and the food was even better than on the *Devonia*, but I had little appetite.

Rebeccca's lovely tear-stained face haunted me wherever I turned. She was always in my dreams, on the pages of my books, and, once, the sight of a young red-haired girl made my heart leap. But, she was not Rebecca.

Rufus was a quick student. By the time we arrived in Chicago he understood the basic physiology and anatomy of the heart and lungs. I asked him about life as a slave, but he preferred to talk about his future in medicine. "I'm gonna set me up an office in Chicago and help all the poor folks who can't afford to go to a fancy white doctor. White. Colored. Chinamen. Indians. Don't matter. I'll give 'em all the best doctoring in the whole state of Illinois."

I scribbled these last notes just as Lake Michigan came into view. The rail line went through the dingiest part of Chicago, but Angus Duncan met us with his gilded grand carriage driven by a smartly uniformed footman. Mr. Duncan had indeed made a great fortune in America. His elegant fawn-colored trousers, dark brown waistcoat, and the heavy gold chain across his vest would made me look like a country bumpkin if it was not for my fine new clothes.

However, Dr. Bell bowed to no man, but greeted his fellow Scot and introduced me as his assistant. Perhaps it was the fine clothes or my Edinburgh education. Either way, I had gained confidence and walked a bit taller.

Rufus sat with the Negro coachman in the driver's seat and we were off through the streets of Chicago. I was dazzled by the new buildings that had been erected in the seven years since the Great Fire. We soon turned onto Prairie Avenue, an elegant tree-lined street with one great mansion after another that had most fortuitously escaped the flames which had devastated so much of this city.

Duncan, like Dr. Bell, was a widower. Once we arrived at his three-story home, built of pink limestone and brick, a maid ushered us into a paneled living room. A lively fire crackled and blazed in a marble fireplace while we had tea and scones and little jam-filled delicacies that reminded me of home.

After tea the two men exchanged stories about their school days, and Mr. Duncan talked about how he had built a great railroad empire in the West and South. They were still talking and having a dram when I went off to my room and fell into a massive four-poster bed.

8 October, 1878

This morning, we went straight to the Chicago County Hospital. The morning clinic in the huge amphitheatre was attended by a few Rush professors and a handful of noisy students. It was only then that I realized American doctors greatly oppose Lister's new antiseptic method. Just as the clinic was about to begin, an angry student shouted, "No women! Get out!" The center of the commotion was a small elegantly dressed woman who beat her assailants back with an umbrella.

Dr. Bell raised his hand. "Behave like gentlemen or this clinic will be terminated. In Edinburgh, I welcome members of the fairer sex interested in the medical arts, and I shall do the same here . . . As should you."

The male students sullenly took their places. Bell offered his hand and escorted the woman to a place in the front row. She was a dark, sensual Mediterranean lass with twinkling grey eyes and black hair. The wrinkles about her eyes and lips did not detract from her beauty. The boys may not have liked women in their classes, but they ogled her attractive figure in tight-fitting skirt and shirtwaist.

"Thank you, Professor. We, in America, admire your courage in teaching female medical students and your interest in the nursing profession. I am Emilie Droussard" she said.

When patients arrived and the clinic started, the students settled into learning and were not so very different from my classmates in Edinburgh.

I took notes as the Rush students presented their cases. There was the usual run of patients with hemorrhoids, broken bones, and consumption, but nothing tested Dr. Bell's acumen until a student wheeled an impish little man of perhaps forty years into the small amphitheatre. He complained of a lump and pain on the right side of his abdomen. The Rush professors had diagnosed a tumor of the kidney.

The patient sat on the edge of his stretcher, dangled his legs, and grinned like a monkey. Dr. Bell looked at him, "Good morning, Mr. Ericsson. I see that you suffered an injury in the recent war."

The man proudly pointed at a scar just to left of center in his chest. "Yes, indeed, it was a Confederate ball. Special delivery on the first day at Shiloh."

"Your rib must have blocked the bullet from your heart."

The patient had a broad smile when he twisted around to show another scar on his back. "Oh no, sir. The ball went all the way through and festered. The surgeon drained a pint of pus and found the bullet." Mr. Ericsson then proudly removed a conical lead bullet from his trousers pocket. "Here it is."

Dr. Bell had the gleam in his eye that I had come to recognize when he was about to spring one of his great surprises.

"Would you be so kind as to stand up and drop your trousers?"

"Excuse me, Doctor. There is a lady present."

"Please. Indulge me, sir."

Ericsson blushed crimson, but dropped his pants.

"Gentlemen, normally the left testicle descends first and hangs lower. Please note that our patient's right testicle hangs lower than the left. This is a sign of situs inversus, a condition in which all organs are reversed. He survived the gunshot wound only because his heart is on his right side rather than the left. His spleen, normally on the left side of his abdomen, is the mass noted on his right." Dr. Bell sat back in his seat, folded his hands and cast an appreciative glance at the woman.

The Rush professor of surgery, Moses Gunn, who had made the diagnosis of a kidney tumor, scowled and rose to examine the patient. He first put his ear to the patient's chest and then minutely felt his abdomen. "Gentlemen, our distinguished guest, Doctor Bell, is correct. I bow to his diagnostic skill."

The students stamped their feet and clapped their hands. Amidst the uproar, a young man entered the amphitheatre and urgently spoke with Dr. Gunn, who then turned to Bell.

"One of our interns, Dr. Murphy, has a patient in the emergency room. Would you care to come along?"

"By all means," Dr. Bell replied.

The patient was a perfect specimen of manhood, certainly no more than twenty-five years old, muscular, and well-formed. Unfortunately, he was quite dead.

"It happened only a few minutes ago. A policeman was investigating a horse theft at a livery stable and he observed the victim walking as normal as could be with a group of men. Then, suddenly, he said, 'Oh,' walked a pace or two more, stumbled, and fell to the ground," Dr. Murphy explained.

During Doctor Murphy's recital of the history, Dr. Bell minutely examined the body. "Were there signs of life when the policeman found him?"

"He was gasping for air and his eyes were wide open. It was as if he was pleading for help. That's why I rushed him to the hospital," the policeman, evidently an experienced detective, replied.

"Is this case similar to other recent deaths in town?"

"Why yes, many of their attributes are the same," Dr. Gunn replied.

"I thought so. The specifics seem to echo the collapsing men mentioned in Angus Duncan's letter which summoned us here. Dr. Gunn, can you arrange for an immediate post-mortem examination?"

The hospital morgue was an ill-lit room in the basement, equipped with a rough wooden table, a tray of rusty instruments, and a bucket of water to sluice away blood.

The body was extraordinarily flaccid and I could not help but notice the victim's open, staring eyes. It was as if he had watched his own death from some faraway place and had begged for mercy.

Dr. Gunn, with practised ease, slit open the body from neck to belly and examined each organ in turn. There was nothing abnormal.

Dr. Bell sniffed at the contents of the stomach which held nothing more than partially digested bits of beef and bread. He then held his chin in one hand and closed his eyes for a long moment. Then to the policeman, he said, "Describe again, in as much detail as possible, your observations."

"It was as I said. The gentleman was walking as normal as any man with a group of friends. When he fell, his friends were immediately upon him, holding his hand and slapping his face. They would have removed his body if I had not found signs of life and insisted on taking him to the hospital."

"And did you observe anything unusual?"

"Not really, but it was a little strange that his friends did not go to the hospital. They abruptly left the scene."

"Did you notice anything else?"

"No, everything seemed perfectly normal . . . Although, there was a lady in black who seemed to be part of the group, but the moment the man fell to the ground, she rushed away."

Dr. Bell offered his hand. "Sir, you have uncommonly good powers of observation."

"Thank you, sir. It is part of our job," said the policeman.

"One more thing, officer. Before you leave would you be so kind as to please turn the body over?" The policeman rolled the corpse onto its stomach.

"Aha, there it is." Dr. Bell pointed to a speck of blood and a puncture wound on the man's left buttock. "This man may have been injected with curare, a deadly South American poison that causes near-instantaneous paralysis and death."

"Are you saying this was murder?" Dr. Gunn asked.

"Indeed, murder most foul."

"But, we must prove it," Doctor Gunn replied.

"Doyle, my instruments, if you please . . ."

I opened the leather case, and, from the rows of gleaming surgical tools, Dr. Bell selected a straight scalpel, forceps, and two hooked retractors. He then, with great care, opened the puncture wound and dissected through the layers until he paused and murmured, "Doyle, hold the tissues apart with retractors."

I separated the skin and fat as he deepened the incision to a layer of muscle at the very end of the wound.

"There," said Dr. Bell. "A few drops of the poison that were not absorbed after death occurred." He selected a glass syringe and drew up the whitish fluid.

"To prove the cause of death, I shall require a small animal. A rabbit or a cat would do nicely."

Within half an hour, two students returned with a sack that contained a writhing, spitting, clawing, grey rat. It was the size of a small cat and rather fearsome-looking. It took two students to hold the rat, a picture of violent activity with ears laid back, until Dr. Bell drove the needle home injecting the deadly white fluid.

Instantly the rodent went limp and collapsed, but, curiously, he struggled to breathe for nearly ten minutes. During this time, his eyes were wide open, and I swear he seemed to be pleading with us to spare his life.

"There, gentlemen—all of the exact symptoms of curare poisoning. The man and the rat died from a lethal dose of this deadly poison used for generations by natives in South America."

That evening, Angus Duncan and Dr. Bell shared a bottle of port. "Angus, your suspicion of foul play in the cases of the collapsing men is well-founded," said Dr. Bell.

"What? How did you know?"

"Your handwriting gave you away. You must insist on a police investigation."

"The Chicago Police are more concerned with taking bribes than investigating crime, but I shall notify the Commissioner. Your help will be most appreciated."

10 November, 1878

Over the course of this last month, I have been busy. So busy that I have failed to record my thoughts in this journal. But, I shall fill in all the blanks of the past few weeks now in these next few pages.

I assisted Dr. Bell as he repaired crooked legs, operated upon joints infected with tuberculosis, and repaired cleft lips. Rufus quickly learned how to clean instruments and swab down the skin of patients with carbolic solution. I have assisted at surgery, and Dr. John Murphy, the delightful, red-haired Irish intern, gave the anaesthetic for all our surgical cases.

At first, only Dr. Gunn and a few students were present, but, as news of Dr. Bell's incredible results with the antiseptic method became known, more and more students and physicians began attending his clinics.

Every single day, Emilie Droussard sat in the front row, avidly taking notes and occasionally asking questions. Dr. Bell seemed to take great delight in her attention. Additionally, by the end of the week even lay people were drawn to witness Dr. Bell's feats of surgical skill.

During the afternoons, Rufus and I had the run of Rush Medical College, which was just across the street from the hospital. Most of the students were rough, uneducated country laddies, but still good fellows.

Beyond the hospital and medical college, it seemed like every other establishment in the city was a saloon, gambling den or brothel. I had no money for gambling and was not interested in the offerings of the painted ladies, since I know too well the horrors of venereal disease. Even when tempted by a particularly attractive wench, the vision of Rebecca's lovely face always appeared to keep me from committing an unspeakable sin.

To-night, after working all day, I invited Rufus to Peachey's Saloon, a good Irish pub that sells an honest mug of ale. A group of Rush Medical College students had congregated there to drink. In the center of a gang of students, an overgrown Wisconsin farm lad by the name of Carl Lindborg was telling stories, to roars of laughter. Over six feet tall, with massive arms and legs, he had a huge head of curly blonde hair, rosy cheeks, and a baby face. As he spoke, he held a lit El Perfecto in the side of his mouth and punctuated the best moments in his story with a wave of the cigar.

I tried to push my way inside the circle around Lindborg. "Excuse me. Pardon me," said I, but nobody budged. Did bringing Rufus make me an outcast?

Lindborg heard my Scottish accent. "I hear that a Scotsman knows how to drink," he barked.

"I was born in Scotland, but have some Irish and English blood, so I wouldn't exactly call myself a Scot. The name's Arthur Conan Doyle."

"Well, Artie . . ."

"The name is Arthur."

He pointed the El Perfecto Cigar. "Whatever you call yourself, my friend, might you be interested in challenging this wee American lad of Swedish descent to a chugging contest?"

"It would be my pleasure to teach you a lesson on how to drink, sir, but I believe it would be more fitting to propose an arm wrestling match instead."

"Even better. I have milked cows my whole life and never lost an arm wrestling match." As the other students laughed and snickered, suddenly the circle around him parted and I was ushered into the center.

Carl and I struggled and grunted and strained for a good minute or two before he bested me. Within five minutes we were smoking cigars together, and I could not help but like this giant of a lad who must not have been more than eighteen.

As Lindborg and I chatted, he continued to imbibe while I smoked deeply on one of his cigars. Next thing I knew, we were discussing the scarcity of bodies for anatomical dissection in Chicago. Our discussion inspired Carl. "Artie, I have me an idea."

"It is Arthur."

"Either way, follow me." He led me and a group of medical students to a uniformed copper sitting on a stool at the far end of the bar. The police officer was eating a late dinner of boiled eggs and a pig's foot.

Lindborg pushed a pint across the bar to the officer. "Paddy, my friend, would you care for a drink?"

"I would not turn down a pint," said the copper.

After Paddy had several mugs of good beer, as well as a dram or two, Lindborg patted his back. "Paddy, my dear old friend, may we borrow your wagon for a bit?"

The policeman nodded and we were off. Carl and his lads stopped at their lodgings to gather spades, shovels, a large canvas bag, a chisel, and a hammer. It appeared as if this was a common student activity. A half-dozen of us, including Rufus, piled into the four-wheeled wagon drawn by one poor horse.

We traveled through the darkened streets, mostly north and east by my calculations, until we were beyond the city limits. As we drew nearer to Lake Michigan a cold rain, driven by a northeast wind, sprung up. We plodded along until a large, decrepit sign announced 'GRACELAND CEMETERY'.

For a moment, I wondered if we were any better than MacLure, the Greyfriars Killer, but then I reasoned that what we were doing could save a good deal of lives. I proceeded along with Lindborg.

Inside this dreary place there appeared to be several acres of gravestones surrounded by a broken down fence. The wind sighing in rows of trees and the patches of fog lent a ghostly aura of gloom. I shivered with cold and had real misgivings about the whole enterprise. "Carl, we shouldn't be doing this."

"Look here, Artie. You can stand there and look down on me from your high and mighty Scottish pulpit, or you can roll up your sleeves and help. Either way, we are going to do this."

"CALL ME ARTHUR! And what if . . ."

"I can't afford to think about what ifs . . . The other medical schools have the money to buy bodies, but, if we want to learn anatomy, it is up to us to provide the specimens. And so, what choice do we have?" said Carl.

Rufus stepped forward, "I'll stand here as your lookout. Mr. Doyle, why don't you stay with me?"

I paused, considered his proposal and sighed. "Alright, then, Rufus and I shall be your lookouts."

Carl and his boys continued until they came to a fresh grave in the pauper's section. With the help of a shaded lantern, the boys set to work shoveling the loose wet dirt until their spades struck the wooden coffin.

I shivered in my bones at the hollow awful sound. It was one thing to dissect a body—an innate thing—beneath a bright light and quite another thing to bring up a fresh corpse from what was supposed to be its final resting place.

The combination of the sighing wind, the flickering lights, the brush of tree limbs, and the shadows playing amongst the statues and gravestones was more than enough to take away my thin veneer of rational scientific thought. Perhaps there really were spirits and ghosts that haunted places such as this.

Lindborg, with practised ease, chiseled off the top of the coffin. The boys removed the body, placed it in the canvas bag, and carried it to the police wagon. The boys passed a bottle to me. I quickly got over my qualms and looked forward to testing my knowledge of anatomy against the Americans.

Within the hour, we returned the wagon to Paddy and the body was safely on the dissecting table in the anatomical laboratory. The corpse was that of a well-dressed, well-formed young man. He was clearly not a pauper. While we removed his clothing, the body was face down on the table. "My God, there is a puncture wound in his left buttock," I gasped.

We then turned the body face up and stepped back in horror. His neck had been slashed from ear to ear, leaving a gaping bloody wound.

It was then I noticed the open, desperate eyes that, though dull and dead, seemed to plead for mercy—just like the rat. There was also the unmistakable odor of carbolic acid about the man's neck.

Carl and the rest of our tipsy companions quickly sobered at the sight of that ghastly slashed throat and the eyes, dulled by death, but still wide open, pleading for an answer as to why he was murdered.

The other students faded away from the dissecting room leaving just me, Carl, and poor Rufus alone with that awful corpse. Before he came to Rush, Carl had been apprenticed to a busy surgeon and had seen his share of wounds and death, so he was not shocked.

He even had the presence of mind to lower the shades and darken the windows. "The murderer would not be happy to know that we have discovered his victim," said he.

At first I did not understand, and then it struck me. When Dr. Bell had made his clever discovery of homicide, he had unwittingly thrust us all into danger. Yes, like it or not, we had stumbled upon a series of dreadful murders and, as a result, we would surely be thrust into a truly perilous game. Truly, "the game was afoot," as Doctor Bell often said.

"Rufus, please fetch Dr. Bell immediately," I said.

11 November, 1878

In the wee hours of the morning, Dr. Bell arrived, accompanied by Angus Duncan. Dr. Bell quietly inspected me and Carl and shook his head disapprovingly. "Doyle. Please remember, we are guests in this country. You must promise to refrain from engaging in unlawful activities," said he.

"Doctor Bell, sorry, sir, but—"

"Robbing graves is a criminal offence."

"Sir", I stammered, "It . . . It was only a prank and the students—they are doing it for the sake of their studies. They need anatomical material."

"Even in the name of medical research, it is still illegal."

"How did you know this cadaver was stolen?"

"Elementary, lad, elementary. 'Tis the power of observation, as I have attempted to instruct you." There was a ghost of a smile on his lips. "Graceland Cemetery is well known for its fine stand of Hazelnut trees and there is a Hazelnut leaf stuck to the underside of your muddy left shoe."

His astounding observational skills once again amazed me. If only I could learn to observe, deduce, and make a correct diagnosis.

Dr. Bell then circled the corpse, observing it with great intensity and sniffing its odors.

Mimicking the technique I had seen Dr. Bell use in the past, I put my chin on my knuckles and studied the cadaver. The body was undressed, but the well-tailored suit of clothes we had removed suggested that he had been a gentleman. Even in death, the facial features were symmetrical, and the body was well-built. Aside from the puncture wound and slashed throat, there were no other outward signs of injury and nothing to indicate that the victim had attempted to defend himself.

"Roll the body over, and a probe, please," Dr. Bell requested.

I handed him an iron probe. The probe entered the puncture wound at a slightly upward angle. The wound appeared to be two inches deep. By measurement, the corpse from the crown of the head to the heels was about five feet ten inches.

"The needle that delivered the poison was thrust from somewhat below the wound in an upward direction, suggesting that the assailant was shorter than the victim," Bell surmised.

After he had minutely inspected the body Dr. Bell turned to the slashed throat. The wound was cleanly incised as if the assailant had used an extraordinarily sharp instrument.

With steel hook retractors, Carl and I separated the edges of the wound. Dr. Bell gasped. "This is no ordinary slashing. The killer was a gifted surgeon who dissected each layer with supreme precision and avoided the great arteries and veins."

We eagerly peered into the wound. "Great God in Heaven! There's no thyroid gland!" Dr. Bell exclaimed.

Indeed, the thyroid gland, a reddish, paired organ shaped like half of a peach, was missing. It normally covered the trachea and the jugular veins, but in this case it was gone. The wind pipe and great veins were uncovered in the depths of the incision, and the vessels that had supplied blood to the gland were now neatly divided.

Mr. Duncan, who had silently held back away from the corpse, finally found his voice. "Who could have committed such a dreadful crime?"

"This was clearly the work of a devilish surgeon. Angus, we must notify the police at once."

"The police have done nothing to investigate the previous cases and I fear they will do nothing about this. Instead, let me send for my good friend, Allan Pinkerton," said Duncan.

Every Scot knew of Pinkerton, a native of Glasgow who founded a famous detective agency. He was a source of national pride because he had once saved Abraham Lincoln from assassination.

Pinkerton arrived in a carriage drawn by four fast horses just after dawn. He was stocky, with a high forehead and a bushy, black beard. He was accompanied by two detectives. After greeting us brusquely he examined the body in minute detail and then took a series of photographs. "Gentlemen," said he, "You are no longer needed. I shall take this case from here."

Dr. Bell and I looked at each other. Duncan jovially clapped Dr. Bell on the shoulder, "That's enough for one evening. Gentlemen, it has been a long night. Let us all repair to the Tremont Hotel for breakfast."

We went off in two carriages. Rufus came along, but refused to enter the dining room. "I'll get me a bite in the kitchen," said he.

The sumptuous dining room, decorated in gold gilt, overlooked Lake Michigan. Carl Lindborg and I were out of place in our shabby clothing and dirty hands, but we took our place at the table and set to work on ham steak, fried eggs, and sweet rolls slathered in butter and jam.

When the party settled down to coffee and morning cigars, Allan Pinkerton tapped his glass for attention. "Gentlemen, to solve this case I need to know as much information as possible, so, at the request of Mr. Duncan, I have decided to hear from our medical colleague, Dr. Joseph Bell."

Dr. Bell, in his usual manner, laced his fingers together over his chest and spoke in his quiet, squeaky voice laced with a wee bit of a Scottish brogue. "We have two victims with similar puncture wounds. In the first, we proved the presence of a poison that caused paralysis and death within a few minutes. The poison was undoubtedly South American curare. The second victim was rendered helpless by the same poison, and, either while still alive, or immediately after his death, the assailant removed his thyroid gland."

"Hmm. Well . . . What, exactly, is the function of this gland?" Allan Pinkerton asked.

"We know very little. However, Swiss surgeons have observed a decline in all body functions, especially intelligence, after the removal of enlarged thyroid glands. The condition resembles cretinism that occurs in children born without a thyroid gland."

"What would be the purpose of removing the gland from an apparently healthy young man?" Angus Duncan asked.

"I have no answer for that. The Swiss have implanted various glands from animals into patients with declining sexual and mental function, but, thus far, their experiments have failed."

When a memory of a lecture by our chemistry professor flashed into my mind, I could not help but add my bit to the conversation. "Sir, at university back in Edinburgh, Professor Brown proposed a series of experiments using fresh extract of the thyroid gland to increase intelligence. Is it possible that this murder is part of such an experiment?"

Dr. Bell glanced my way with fresh interest. "Doyle, my lad, you may have hit upon a motive, but I believe it is still far too early for us to know for sure. What we do know is this. The perpetrator is undoubtedly a well-trained surgeon with a detailed knowledge of chemistry. His use of carbolic acid indicates that he wanted to keep the gland free from infection for some as-yet-unknown use."

I was across the table from Pinkerton and Bell, who were sitting together. The detective's expression went from concentration and interest to a rather condescending smile and annoyance. "Professor Bell, you and your assistant may thrive in the world of academia, but detective work is a bloody and dangerous game that provides little room for a bookish gent such as yourself. I thank you and now hope that you will stick to your ivory tower and let me and my agency do what we are famous for."

A crimson blotch rose on Doctor Bell's cheeks, and he stabbed the air with his long, delicate index finger. "First of all, let me point out that one person could not have poisoned the victims and carried off their bodies alone. There must have been a gang. And sir, don't you at least want to know how the poison was delivered?"

"Ah yes, you have a theory about that, as well, I presume."

"I do, indeed."

"Well, let's have it."

"A hollowed out walking stick, or, perhaps, an umbrella with a plunger connected to a retractable needle at the tip of the stick, could easily deliver the poison. A type of *sword cane*, if you will. The victim would be unaware of his assailant's approach until he felt the prick of the needle, and then it would be too late." As he spoke, Dr. Bell jabbed Mr. Pinkerton in the back with his index finger.

Pinkerton jumped to his feet, "Touch me again, sir, and I shall break that finger of yours!"

"Sir," Dr. Bell smiled gently. "I was merely demonstrating the murderer's technique."

I had, during the conversation, been idly looking about the room and spotted a woman wearing a flowery hat. Her face was hidden by the hat and a newspaper. When Dr. Bell spoke she crumpled the paper, and I had a glimpse of her black curly hair and worried eyes. She looked like the woman who had attended Dr. Bell's clinics, but, before I could make out her features, she turned away and hurriedly left the dining room.

A tall, distinguished man with a droopy mustache and greying hair met her at the door. They paused long enough for me to see that he was wearing a grey suit with a decoration in his lapel. She carried an umbrella even though the day promised fair weather.

Refreshed by the meal and several cups of strong coffee, we left for the medical school with Angus Duncan.

"Angus, I fear that Mr. Pinkerton cares little for our observations," Dr. Bell mused.

"He does things his own way. He and his agents have solved many crimes involving train robberies and counterfeiting; however, he is still smarting from his failure to capture the notorious James Gang."

The day's clinic began with the usual bustle of house officers (what the Americans termed "interns") and students, arriving to take their places in the theatre. There was more than the usual interest today because the patient was a young woman with a tumor on the side of her face. Several local surgeons had declared her beyond help.

Carl, Rufus, and I scrubbed with greater care than usual to remove the grave dirt from our hands, and Dr. Bell insisted that we wear a clean butcher's apron over our clothing. Unruly students were noisily shelling and munching on peanuts in the back row until Dr. Bell shot them a stony glance. He never tolerated nonsense from students—whether in Edinburgh or America. When he removed his frock coat and rolled up the sleeves of his white shirt, several older surgeons guffawed.

"Are you not afraid of soiling your white shirt?" one of the surgeons asked.

"Better to soil one's shirt than the wound," Dr. Bell answered.

The operation was long and intricate, since Bell had to dissect the tumor without damaging the nerves that controlled facial expression. After he was done, and when the girl had awakened from the ether, Dr. Bell sighed with visible relief. He then answered questions concerning the antiseptic method.

It was not the first time that he lingered after a clinic to talk with Emilie Droussard. He seemed quite charmed by the twinkle-eyed lady. I overheard her say that she was anxious to introduce a Nightingale type of nursing service to a hospital. I did not catch the name of the city.

We were both dead-tired, but Carl was eager to dissect the cadaver. Several students had already opened the abdomen under the watchful eyes of Dr. Gunn, but the intestine had gone putrid and, despite wreaths of tobacco smoke, the smell was overpowering.

Several students were especially keen to dissect the intricate plexus of nerves in the neck that led to the arm. Rufus seemed oblivious to the smell and eagerly followed our work, asking questions all the while. Carl and I took turns poking and cutting into the body.

Sadly, muscles and nerves are never as clear as depicted in a book. We first stripped away the skin and then separated muscles and dissected beneath the clavicle.

I set out to display the origin of the median nerve with a great deal of confidence, but the scalpel and forceps soon became slippery with fat and, for a while, I was hopelessly lost. Together, Carl and I finally found the junction of the medial and lateral cords of the brachial plexus that formed the median nerve. It was then easy to trace the median nerve in its course next to the humerus bone.

The dissection had taken so long that most of the students had drifted away. It was early evening before we decided to have a beer and a bite to eat at Peachey's Saloon. Just as Rufus went off to visit his new friends at the Tremont Hotel, the dean of the medical school thrust a letter in my hand. The name, Rebecca Yates, was on the envelope, and my heart soared.

I wanted to tear open the envelope, but decided to wait until I could savour her words in the quiet of my room. Carl loitered to clean and put away his dissecting instruments while I left the building with my mind on Rebecca.

There was the sound of hurrying footsteps, and I was dimly aware of something moving in the periphery of my vision. But, when I halted, scanned the street, and listened, I did not see anything in the gathering darkness. I should have waited for Carl, but memories of Rebecca's kiss had overtaken my senses.

I paused in the midst of my fantasy. The street was suddenly silent, deadly silent. Why had I walked out alone?

In a moment of terror, I remembered Dr. Bell's theory of the walking stick filled with poison and started to run.

Hands grabbed me. Sharp pain shot through my arms and back. It was not the sting of a needle. Ruffians wrenched my arms behind my back and forced me to the ground. I struggled until rough hands held a cloth soaked in chloroform over my face.

I fought against the sweet fumes. And from a great distance heard I a soft, melodic American-accented voice, "Take care. He will make a fine specimen."

12 November, 1878

Early this morning, I woke up and thanked God that I was still alive. I was in Carl Lindborg's bed. He was sleeping on the floor next to me. When he saw me trying to get out of bed he jumped up. "Artie, please –" said he.

"It is Arthur."

"Either way, don't get up too quickly. Just sit back and tell me what you remember."

Through a chloroform haze, I told him that I recalled bits and pieces of my attempted abduction—rough hands dragging me, my heels bumping on the cobblestones, flashes of light, someone screaming, fists flying, shouts, curses.

Carl half-carried half-led me through the streets of Chicago to Angus Duncan's house and into his parlor. I was still groggy and had only partially regained my senses. Dr. Bell and several other gentlemen from Rush Medical College were having breakfast together when we arrived.

"Good heavens. What happened?" Angus asked.

I told them what I could of the moments before being overcome by the chloroform. Carl stepped in and told them how he had finished his work, and, fortunately, emerged from the dissecting room just in time to see two thugs drag me across the road to a four-horse carriage.

He screamed and tackled one of my assailants, but the other knocked him to his knees with a terrific blow to the back of the head from a stout, gilded cane. Carl went down screaming, "Help! Murder! Police!"

There were no police, but a group of medical students leaving Peachey's Saloon ran to our rescue and swarmed around the thugs. After an exchange of kicks and blows they dragged me from the carriage and pulled Carl back onto his feet. Then, the coachman whipped up the horses, the thugs jumped on, and the carriage rushed away from the scene.

Angus Duncan put down his china tea cup. "These days in Chicago, I have heard of more than one instance of thieves using chloroform on their victims," said he.

"However, these do not sound like common thieves, sir, for when was the last time you have heard of ruffians having a four-horse carriage?" Dr. Gunn interjected.

In his usual way, Dr. Bell asked a penetrating question. "Mr. Lindborg, please try to remember—and do be specific—did you see anything different or unusual about the carriage?"

Carl rubbed his forehead and thought for a moment. "It was very dark, but it seemed to be an uncommonly fine gold-leafed carriage with spirited horses."

"Did you hear anything?"

"The thugs cursed, and at least one student cried out when he was struck down. Amid it all, I do seem to remember a woman's voice from within the carriage."

A dim memory stirred. "Yes, I heard her say the words, *'Take care. He will make a fine specimen,'*" said I.

"Just before the coach drove away I also heard someone saying a general would be damn angry. It could have been a woman's voice. I'm not sure. If those goons hadn't attacked me from behind, I swear I could have taken them all." Carl added.

"Doctor Bell, Is this episode related to those two recent deaths and your theory of murder by poisoning?" Dr. Gunn asked.

Dr. Bell mused, "Well, one need not rush to any conclusions. All one can do is try to separate the probable from the possible and the impossible."

"In that case, what do you find to be probable?"

"Ahem . . . I do think it is fair for one to conclude the following. The term 'specimen' is an unusual one to be used in the context of a common robbery, but not unusual for use in a scientific experiment. For example, Doyle is similar in stature and age to the two recent victims. Angus, tell us, what were the physical characteristics of the first two victims?"

Angus pondered a moment. "By Jove, they were both well-built men, of about the same stature and age as young Doyle."

"Were autopsies performed?" Dr. Bell asked.

"Relatives took charge of the bodies even as they lay on the street. There wasn't a funeral, as far as I can remember, because the men lived in a different city."

"Would it be difficult to exhume the bodies? I believe these murders are the work of a well-trained surgeon," Dr. Bell said.

"I cannot believe that anyone in the medical profession would murder in cold blood for the purpose of removing an organ," Dr. Gunn replied.

"The case of Dr. Corcoran in Edinburgh, who paid for the bodies of recently murdered victims for anatomical dissection, was not so terribly different. He defended his actions by claiming that, since the victims were already dead, he could use them for teaching anatomy, thereby benefitting humanity," Dr. Bell said.

Dr. Isham, a professor of medicine at Rush, spoke for the first time. "That reminds me of Dr. Eli McGillicutty who grafted skin onto burn victims after the fire of '71."

"What ever happened to McGillicutty?" Dr. Bell asked.

"There was a great scandal when he experimented with grafting animal skin onto humans. All of his patients died. Some called it murder. He claimed it was to advance science, but county commissioners removed him from the hospital staff. McGillicutty has since disappeared," Dr. Isham replied.

The meeting broke up and the doctors went their separate ways. Doctor Bell was to present another clinic. "Doyle, my boy, you have had a difficult, perilous night," said Dr. Bell. "Take today off and rest until you feel up to snuff. Oh, and here is five dollars. You have more than earned it."

I was grateful for the chance to rest, but, even after several cups of hot tea and generous helpings of eggs and ham, I still felt awful and went to my room. I was too restless to sleep and tried to read my medical textbooks for an hour or two, but I could not get Dr. Eli McGillicutty out of my mind. He sounded exactly like the sort of physician who might experiment on human beings. The idea of human experimentation was deeply disturbing, especially when I considered that I just narrowly escaped being the subject of just such an experiment.

But, then, we would not have anaesthetics, ether, and chloroform if doctors had not experimented on medical students and taken the drugs themselves.

I am venturing deeper and deeper into the heart of this mystery and this great, enigmatic American nation. I am filled with questions. Much of what I have always thought of as absolute in my life is beginning to shift and alter. What is right and what is wrong no longer seem as clear to me as they once did.

As I set down these events of the past few days, I realize we are embroiled in a complex mystery. Even Dr. Bell does not seem to have any answers. With those confused thoughts, I am finally ready to drift off to sleep.

13 November, 1878

Bright sun was streaming through the windows when I awoke. It was early in the morning and I must have slept a good ten hours . . .

And I must have been dreaming about skin grafting for burns because the idea of it popped into my mind as soon as I was awake. Out of what I justified as professional curiosity, I was determined to learn more about Dr. McGillicutty.

"Where can one find old newspaper stories?" I asked the cook during a grand breakfast in the kitchen.

"Ask at the Tribune downtown," she answered.

It was a cold day, but clear and brisk and good for a walk. So, I strolled north on Prairie Avenue with the railroad tracks and chuffing trains close by. Horse-drawn trams, hacks, and wagons of all description filled the bustling streets. Workmen were busily erecting new homes and buildings as high as six stories. A fellow on the street said they were planning one that would go up to eight stories and have a steam elevator. But, since Chicago is so flat there, were no interesting vistas, and my view of the lake was perpetually blocked by tall buildings.

My thoughts turned to my beloved Edinburgh. From almost any street in *Auld Reekie*, one may view a heathery shoulder of the Pentland Hills or glimpse a ship tacking down the Firth of Forth to the North Sea. Aye, perhaps I was homesick. It was just that the new buildings in Chicago did not have the character of our Parliament or St. Giles, and there was nothing so fine in all of Chicago as the statue of Charles the Second astride his charger.

Finally, I reached the Tribune building just off State Street. The lobby was grand, with brass railings and gas lights. I found a clerk wearing a green visor behind a desk. The worthless scamp ignored me for a good while. "Where I might find old copies of papers?" I asked.

"In the archives," said he.

"And where might the archives be?"

The smirking rascal ignored my question until I leaned over the desk and flexed a muscle. "Through that door, down to the basement. If you can't locate what you're looking for, ask for a drunken gent by the name of Fogarty," he finally answered.

I went down smooth, worn, stone stairs to the dingy basement. The sign on the door said 'Archives.' I proceeded through a dark corridor to a dim, musty room filled with stacks and stacks of newspapers and folders filled with clippings. I made my way through the jumble and came to a desk lit with a green oil lamp. Behind the desk was a gnome of a man with a small head of thick brown hair. He shuffled papers with hands as delicate as a child's.

I cleared my throat. "Are you Mr. Fogarty?"

"And, what in hell do you want?" was his reply.

"Um, eh, well . . . Information on a doctor by the name of McGillicutty."

"And who in the name of hell are you?"

"Doyle. I am a visiting medical student from University of Edinburgh."

The gnome cackled with laughter. "I might have known . . . Doyle, eh? Irish, are you?"

"My father is of Irish descent."

"And, I suppose you are a good Catholic."

"I was raised Catholic."

He cackled again, "And, now, you're a damn backslider. I suppose you take a drop now and then."

I did not respond.

The little man pulled a bottle from his desk drawer, took a generous swig and pushed the bottle across his littered desk. "Have a pull and then we shall see about Dr. McGillicutty."

"Thanks, but, no thanks." I wanted to keep clear head.

"More for me, then. Yes, I have information on every damn politician, business man, and half the crooks in town. You can't tell one from another and, yes, there is a file on McGillicutty. I know that bastard well."

When Fogarty rose from his chair, he was less than five feet tall, but he quickly skipped through the stacks of newspapers and returned with a folder. His small stature reminded me of my mate Jimmie Barrie from university. Then, I remembered Dr. Bell's statement that the assailant in the poisoning cases was of small stature. "Have you had any medical training, sir?"

"Hell, no. Studied literature at Oberlin . . . Lot of good it did me."

"I see . . . Um, eh . . . This must be a dismal place to work."

"Ach, you get used to it."

He cleared a space beneath the oil lamp and spread out a series of clippings and advertisements. The first story, dated November 1871, described Dr. McGillicutty's remarkable results in the treatment of burn victims. A brief biography listed him as an 1860 graduate of the Eclectic Scientific Medical School in Nashville, Tennessee where he had won the prize for anatomical dissections. Next, he was a surgeon to the Confederate Army. In 1863, he had resigned from the Army to study in Paris and Vienna.

A photograph showed Dr. McGillicutty wearing a formal suit of clothes and a black silk hat. He had a thick black mustache. Gold-rimmed spectacles were perched on a thin, almost aristocratic nose. He appeared to be highly respectable and the sort of practitioner that one could trust with his life. He also appeared to be of short stature . . .

There was another article about his dismissal from the County Hospital. An advertisement, dated 1874, included a close-up photograph of his face and head without the hat. He was balding and his spectacles were perched lower on his nose. He still appeared to be a solid practitioner, but something was a bit askew about his eyes.

Dr. McGillicutty, in the advertisement, offered the highest quality drugs: cocaine, opium, quinine, digitalis, and extracts of all known plant remedies. The next advertisement was more interesting.

REJUVENATION THERAPY

DR. MCGILLICUTTY'S GLANDULAR EXTRACT

REVIVES SPIRITS, RESTORES YOUTH

&

INCREASES PASSION IN BOTH SEXES

When I saw the word 'glandular' my heart skipped a beat. I hurriedly recorded the information in my notebook, drew a rough sketch of the doctor, and pushed the folder back to Fogarty. "Where is this Dr. McGillicutty now?"

"Ah ha, aren't you the nosey bugger? Any more intelligence will cost you a drink, sonny boy."

Fortunately, Dr. Bell had given me the five dollars, so I could afford a few drinks. His destination, Hinky Dink McKenna's Saloon, was several blocks away in a shabbier part of town. On the way there we passed several mansions where young men and well-dressed young ladies were coming and going. Piano music and feminine laughter filtered out through open doors even though it was the middle of the day.

"Are there always parties here?" I asked.

"Aye, this is Mother Brigit's." He paused for a moment and pointed to an especially gaudy mansion. "The finest sporting house in the world. You can hire a young virgin or an experienced older vixen to teach you the ways of the world. Take your pick."

Hinky Dink's Saloon was a big raucous tavern with a long mahogany bar, scratched wooden tables, sawdust on the floor, and dozens of men lifting a glass. We had no more than arrived at a spot on the bar next to the lunch counter when the barkeeper slid a double shot of whisky to Fogarty, who downed the liquor with one gulp. I had a beer, and we helped ourselves to free pickles and tasty roast beef sandwiches.

He showed no sign of intoxication, but, when he commenced talking about Dr. McGillicutty, he nearly shouted. "McGillicutty, the bastard, promised that if I took ten bottles of his medicine I would grow a half-foot taller and be able to please a woman all night long. The damn stuff didn't work, but he claimed he was brewing a new formula just for me."

Several men put down their drinks and cocked an ear in our direction. "Where is Dr. McGillicutty now?" I asked.

A crafty smile came over his face. "Well, ain't that a bit of a secret?"

"Please, I must know."

He looked at me for a moment and then relented. "I happen to know he has his own private hospital."

"Where?"

"It's in one of me files, somewhere in the archives. Come back to-morrow with a bit of cash and I'll have the address for you."

I reached for money to pay for our drinks and felt Rebecca's letter. How could I have forgotten?

I tossed some coins on the bar, ran into the street, and, with great care, slit open the envelope with my pen knife. I scanned the single page with her delicate writing and then read it through a half-dozen times.

Dear Mr. Doyle,

I must thank you again for your kind assistance and pray that this finds you in good health. The Reverend Balfour is regaining his strength and has had no more spells. We are staying with the Reverend Beecher, a very famous minister who was a good friend of President Lincoln. His sister wrote the story **Uncle Tom's Cabin**.

The Reverend Beecher is a strange man for being a minister, since he was involved in a scandal and was accused of seducing young women in his parish. Of course, these malicious allegations are false. He is a kind man who treats me with great sympathy, almost fondness, but he has changed his opinion about slavery and now believes, like the Reverend Balfour, that the black people should not have been freed. Sadly, his health is failing and I am not sure how much longer he will be of this world.

Now, I have exciting news. Since the Reverend Balfour is feeling better, next week we shall travel to Memphis. Perhaps we shall meet again there after all.

Sincerely Yours,

Rebecca Yates

In the letter, there was not a word expressing any feelings for me. My world turned upside down. I folded the letter, tucked it my notebook, and turned back to the saloon. I wanted to get dead drunk, but the vivid image of my own father lying drunk on the floor crossed my mind. Shame and anger welled up in me. I refused to ever become like him.

Maybe I should just go to a sporting house and find out what it's really like to enjoy the pleasures of the flesh. But, Dr. Bell would not approve. Why should he? He is so different than me. Everything has been so easy for him. He comes from long line of medical aristocrats. His father was a third generation physician, while my father, a struggling artist, has never had a tuppence to his name.

However, it is also true that Dr. Bell has not lived without suffering. He lost his wife and his only son, yet he has never veered from his life's course. When I thought about that, I knew I must do the same. I lifted my shoulders and decided that I will NOT be deterred from a career in medicine by one small setback. I am done with feeling sorry for myself and with romantic yearnings. Miss Rebecca Yates can dally with her elderly minister all she wishes. I am through with her.

14 November, 1878

Immediately after Dr. Bell's morning clinic we went to the children's ward to select patients for surgery to-morrow. The young physician, John Murphy, pushing a dressing cart, led us on rounds, giving a brief history of each of the sick little patients.

Even though the hospital is relatively new, the ward was damp and chilly. Columns blocked light from dirty windows. Dr. Bell clucked at lazy slatterns who swept dirt into corners or under beds, but he tousled the hair and joked with small lads and complimented the girls.

Boys and girls were not separated on the ward, and most beds had at least two small occupants. Apparently there was little interest in children or their diseases because, aside from Dr. Murphy, Carl Lindborg and Rufus, there was only one physician present on the floor.

More than once, Dr. Bell raised his eyebrows. "All this poor child needs is fresh air, sunshine, and good clean milk," he said. Yet these items seemed to be in short supply. At least half of the children suffered from tuberculosis of the bone or lymph glands, and the rest had broken bones from being kicked by a horse or run over by an omnibus.

For surgery the next day, the professor selected a child with tuberculosis of the spine and a large abscess, and another whose chest was filled with fluid, collapsing the lung. I knew he would save both lives.

My feelings about Bell keep shifting. In Edinburgh, he seemed to take pleasure in ridiculing me and I had wanted to curse at him. Now I see that his hard veneer is merely a necessary coat of armour to protect a sensitive disposition. Do all physicians have to harden their hides to survive? I wonder if I can develop the necessary toughness to carry on as a doctor . . .

I said nothing for fear of antagonizing my new friends, but I could not help thinking that a rich country like America must learn to take better care of these poor sick children. Scotland is an old, poor country, but there has never been a speck of dirt on the floors of the Royal Infirmary.

Near the middle of the ward, we came upon a girl of perhaps three years of age who was breathing with terrible difficulty. Her little chest caved in each time she attempted to draw in air, and her lips and fingernails were dusky blue.

"This little one is suffering with the croup," said Dr. Murphy, just as the child gave up her struggle and stopped breathing.

Dr. Bell fixed his eyes on the dying child. "Her vocal cords are completely obstructed. Mr. Doyle, my straight bistoury, please."

I desperately looked at Rufus. I thought he had brought the instruments. He had assumed that I had them. I could barely get the words out. "I'm sorry sir; the instrument case must be in the clinic."

Bell's voice was filled with venom. "You left the instruments?!"

"Aye sir. I'm terribly sorry."

"Then at least find me some carbolic acid, PLEASE!"

I sprinted through the ward until I found a vial of carbolic and then ran back to Dr. Bell with it. Without another word, he removed a small silver pocket knife from his vest pocket and cleaned it with the carbolic.

Then, with no hesitation, he held the child's chin back with one hand and, with the other, sliced an incision down the middle of her neck. Black sticky blood oozed from the wound. With another stroke, he cut into the child's windpipe and twisted the blade to separate the tracheal cartilages.

Dr. Murphy stepped forward and mopped a glob of mucous away with a bit of gauze. The child's chest heaved. She took in a lungful of air through the opening and coughed out plugs of mucous. Her breathing settled down, and, like a miracle, color came back to her cheeks. Murphy ran to obtain a proper tracheotomy tube.

Dr. Bell rarely became angry, but, in this instance, he was steaming. He cuffed my shoulder with an open hand. "Mr. Doyle, at the very least I expect my clerks to be dependable. This child might have died because of your negligence!"

I left to fetch the instrument case. By the time I returned, he had settled down and was discussing the treatment of esotropia (the condition of being cross-eyed) with Dr. Murphy and the physician who had tagged along. I had some interest in eye diseases and listened intently, then thought of the spectacles perched on the nose of Dr. Eli McGillicutty and the slightly off-center appearance of his eyes.

After we had finished the rounds I screwed up my courage to speak. "Sir, I may have information on the murder cases."

"Doyle, I would prefer that you concentrate on assisting me only in the care of medical patients. Please, do not let your concern about crime interfere with your medical duties. Mr. Duncan is having second thoughts about our involvement in this crime. I shall be having lunch with him shortly."

Damn him! Bloody Dr. Bell could drop the case, but I was not going to go away so easily. I was determined to find the wretches who had attempted to kidnap me and learn more about skin grafting.

I saw the doctor off in a cab to his lunch. With great trepidation, I turned the damned instrument case over to Rufus with strict instructions for him to immediately go to Mr. Duncan's home.

The horse drawing the omnibus was spavined and limped on its hind leg. The driver used his whip, but it was not until mid-afternoon that I arrived at the Chicago Tribune building. I immediately went to the basement archives only to find Fogarty asleep in his chair behind his desk. I cleared my throat. "Mr. Fogarty . . . It is I, Doyle. We have an appointment," I announced.

He opened his eyes and gave me a bleary look. "Doyle? I don't know any Doyle. Who the hell are you?"

"Sir, you promised to give me information on the whereabouts of Dr. Eli McGillicutty if I returned today with some cash."

"Are you a damned spy—a damned bloody Pinkerton?"

"No sir. I am Dr. Joseph Bell's medical clerk."

"Oh, you are with Ding Dong Bell." His witticism sent him into cackles of laughter and he seemed to wake up. "That mad Scottish quack."

"Please, you were to tell me about Dr. Eli McGillicutty's whereabouts?"

"You should ask the Colonel down South in the red house. I don't remember—"

"Mr. Fogarty, does this help you remember?" I held out a two-dollar gold piece. His eyes cleared, and he opened a drawer filled with empty bottles. "Damn, I can't think without some whisky. If you want me to find McGillicutty's damn bloody file, go around the corner and fetch me a bottle. "

I purchased a pint of Old Crown and hurried back. I could not have been gone more than half an hour, but, when I returned, the archives section was pitch dark. I struck a wooden lucifer friction match against the brick wall and made my way, step by careful step, through the corridor.

When the friction match spluttered out, I bumped into Fogarty's desk. I lit another match, and, in the flickering yellow light, I saw Fogarty sleeping with his head down on his desk. The oil lamp had been knocked over.

I lifted the lamp out of a pool of what looked like oil and then realized there was dark blood all over the desk. I dropped the whisky bottle and touched Fogarty's neck. He was not asleep, but, quite . . . Dead.

Something protruded from his mouth. "Holy God!" I uttered, and stepped back from the desk just as the lucifer match burned my fingers and flickered out.

I stumbled my way back up the corridor and into the front office of the paper. "Murder! There's been a murder!" I hollered at the top of my lungs.

The next minutes passed in terrible confusion. One of the clerks went into the archives with a lantern, returned immediately, and vomited on the floor. In the chaos that followed, there were screams for police. "Notify Mr. Medill!" someone yelled.

Within minutes, two constables arrived on the scene. After being equipped with lanterns they went into the basement. I followed and beheld an awful spectacle. Fogarty's chin rested on the edge of the desk and a long knife protruded from his mouth.

Lamp oil and blood soaked the papers on the desk. One constable reached for the knife. "I don't think we should touch anything," I warned.

The constables, more accustomed to dealing with vagrants and drunks than murder, readily agreed, and we returned to the first floor. The clerk, who yesterday had directed me to the archives, pointed in my direction. "There, that man. He is the murderer!"

The constables drew their revolvers and pinioned me against a large marble column, pulling my arms back and applying handcuffs. I was the victim of rough frontier justice—tried, sentenced, and executed by the mob before I had a chance to prove my innocence.

Fortunately for my health and longevity, a distinguished bearded gentleman, dressed entirely in black and wearing a silk top hat, had entered the room and quickly restored order. Much to my surprise, he was accompanied by Angus Duncan and Dr. Bell.

The gentleman was named Mr. Joseph Medill. He was the owner and publisher of the Tribune and had been the Mayor of Chicago after the Great Fire. He had been having a long lunch with Duncan and Bell at the Union League Club when he was summoned.

The constables described the scene in the basement, but their English was rather poor and the powers of observation were even poorer. "Fetch Allan Pinkerton," Medill ordered, after listening a moment.

Then, Mr. Duncan asked that I be released. Dr. Bell drew me aside. "Doyle, what in God's good name is the meaning of this?" he whispered.

I quickly explained my interest in Dr. McGillicutty and locating the newspaper file. "The murdered man is in the basement." I said.

Mr. Medill, sweeping his cane from side to side, quickly cleared the room. "I should've fired the damned Irish drunkard long ago! And the damn democrats had a hand in this, I will wager."

Medill was still ranting when Allan Pinkerton arrived. "Who found the body?" he demanded. I stepped forward.

"Lead the way," he commanded.

During the hour or so since I had found the body, blood had congealed on the desk, but nothing else had changed. Mr. Pinkerton was about to remove the murder weapon. "May I examine the body?" Dr. Bell asked.

Pinkerton stepped in front of Bell. "The man is clearly dead. A doctor's opinion would be of no use now."

"I disagree." Dr. Bell stepped around Pinkerton, wrapped a handkerchief about the hilt of the knife, and gently moved it back and forth; the head moved with the blade since it was solidly imbedded. "The murder weapon entered slightly from the left of his mouth, went through the back of the throat, and is imbedded in the vertebra. From the volume of blood, I would wager that the tip of the blade severed the right vertebral artery. He may have temporarily recovered from the initial shock of the blow, only to die when he strangled on his own blood."

I held the grisly head while Allan Pinkerton used all his strength to remove the knife, which he identified as a bayonet, with the letters C.S.A. stamped on the blade.

"Have not seen one of these since the war," said Pinkerton.

"What does it stand for?" I asked.

"Confederate States of America."

Mr. Pinkerton seemed to have completed his investigation and, after wrapping the bayonet wrapped in cloth, he left the scene.

Dr. Bell motioned me to stay. "Look at this," said he.

Fogarty had scrawled something in his own blood on the desk top. The words were nearly illegible, but they seemed to say *cinnte faoi ghlas*.

I wanted to solve the mystery right then and there, but Dr. Bell urged me to return post haste to the hospital and take over the care of the little girl with the croup.

Her breathing was still labored and her big brown eyes reminded me of my little sister, Ida. As she coughed and struggled for air, I knew something had to be done for her. I devised a method to aspirate her trachea using a syringe and a tube and, after a while, she took some broth and bits of bread. Her breathing sounded much better, and I felt good about being able to help her.

When Dr. Murphy arrived to take over her care just before midnight, she was peacefully asleep. As I walked home, I realized that I was able to perform the aspiration without freezing up. Was it because the little girl reminded me of my little sister, Ida, or that Dr. Bell was not watching, or that I did not think about any of it, I just acted?

I shall never know. But, for the first time in a long time, I thought that maybe, just maybe, I might become a tolerable physician.

When I returned to our lodgings, to my surprise Dr. Bell was still awake and going over his notes. I expected another severe chastisement. Instead, he invited me into his room and motioned to a chair next to his blazing fire.

He poured out a dram of sherry for himself. "I know this might sound redundant, but, now, please indulge me and tell me everything that happened between you and this man Fogarty."

I started from the beginning and told him everything, from the time the thugs accosted me outside of the anatomy lab to my conversations with Fogarty. I showed him the sketches I had made of Dr. McGillicutty. Doctor Bell grunted his approval and leaned back in his chair with his right fist under his chin. He tapped the sketch of McGillicutty. "Pinkerton suspects this man has connections to the foreign socialists who are intent on destroying Mr. Duncan's railroads by murdering his employees. He may be our man."

"But, only the first two victims were employed by Mr. Duncan," said I.

"That's true, but we don't know anything about the most recent victims. Now, tell me in more detail anything that you have not mentioned about the events of today."

"Well, Fogarty seemed to hate the Pinkertons and he said something strange along the lines of, 'Ask the Colonel down South in the red house . . . ' I could make nothing of it. But, I do believe the words he wrote in his own blood are Gaelic."

I passed the page of my notebook with the words *cinnte faoi ghlas.*

"Aye, indeed. One would tend to think that he would write in his native tongue during his last moments. I shall have a chat with Mrs. O'Flynn as to their meaning."

At the mention of the cook's name I wondered what delicacies might be in the kitchen. I had missed dinner again. She had promised roast duck with orange sauce, but, due to the awful events that I had been involved in on this day, I ended up going to bed hungry.

And now, I cannot sleep . . .

So here I am, writing this entry to try to get my mind off my growling stomach. I came on this little adventure to see America, but I never dreamed that my life would almost be snuffed out by thugs or that I would be involved in solving a series of murders!

What have I gotten myself into? When Bell asked me to accompany him I should have flatly refused. Aye, my family is poor, but back in Scotland I was safe and happy and my stomach was always full. AND no one was trying to kill me. Maybe I am not cut out for a life of adventure, after all.

15 November, 1878

I awoke this morning, hungry as a bear, with no thoughts at all about my grim musings of the past night.

The morning operating clinic went quickly, and, after the usual discussion, Dr. Bell announced that he was about to perform a post-mortem examination on an interesting case. Word had gotten about that Fogarty was to be the subject.

There was a rumble of displeasure and almost-lewd remarks when Emilie Droussard insisted on remaining to witness the post mortem examination, but Bell silenced them with a hiss and a wave of his hand.

The diener rolled the corpse, covered with a sheet, into the amphitheatre while Bell arranged his instruments. The audience was silent when Bell drew back the covering and revealed Fogarty's body, which was the size of a small, hairless lad with undeveloped genitalia. Fogarty's lips were drawn back in a rictus of terror and his eyes were wide open.

"Gentlemen, you will agree that we have a most unusual case. This man, nearly forty years of age, has a body which has not developed beyond childhood. Our task is to determine the cause of this condition."

Bell made an incision from the neck to the pubis and quickly dissected the organs, which he placed on a pan beside the body. The heart, lungs, and stomach were perfectly normal, but the liver was in the advanced stages of alcoholic cirrhosis.

He then carefully placed the testicles, adrenal gland, and the thyroid on the pan and pointed to each with the tip of his knife. "Observe, these glands, the ones that we believe regulate the body—are atrophic."

Bell turned his attention to the gruesome head with the open mouth and congealed blood on the lips and gums. "Now, we will see a most rare abnormality of the pituitary gland."

He rolled the head from side to side. "What have we here?" He pulled the hair aside and demonstrated a smear of blood around a small hole in the back of the head. "It is a puncture wound."

He then drew his long, razor-sharp knife across the back of the head, from ear to ear and rolled the scalp back over the forehead, so that, when replaced, the face would appear to be untouched. Whatever instrument had made the puncture wound had penetrated deeply into the skull. "Doyle, look here." With the tip of his knife, he removed a small fragment of metal imbedded in the skull. "Take this and keep quiet," he whispered in my ear.

I palmed the bit of metal, turned my back to the crowd, and slipped it inside my billfold.

Bell then sawed through the circumference of the skull and removed the skull cap, revealing the glistening brain with its convolutions, sulci, and veins. The physicians and students in the audience leaned forward with rapt attention. Perhaps some of them had never seen a human brain before.

Emilie Droussard's delicate features were deathly pale. I was surprised because she had witnessed operations and organ removal with equanimity, and I did not expect her to appear affected.

Bell then removed the brain, and, with infinite care, dissected the pituitary gland and held it up for all to see. "As anticipated, the pituitary gland, the supreme regulator of the body, has failed to develop. This undoubtedly caused Mr. Fogarty's small stature."

"Gentlemen, come, I want all of you to see the small size of the sella turcica, where the pituitary gland normally resides. Older textbooks refer to this saddle-like depression in the sphenoid bone as a 'Turkish chair.' "

When the crowd moved in closer to Fogarty's body, Emilie Droussard quietly left. Out of curiosity, I followed her out to the street.

She was adjusting her shawl, not far away, when a stooped, sallow-faced fellow came up to me. "You are one of the doctors caring for my little girl in the children's ward. I can't thank you enough."

"You should thank Dr. Bell. He was the one who saved her life."

The man poked his head close to mine. "I was in Hinky Dink's Saloon when I overheard your conversation with Fogarty. Since you helped my little Gracie, I kin tell ya this. If you want Dr. McGillicutty, there he goes." He pointed at a man walking in the opposite direction down the street.

"Damn," I thought. McGillicutty had been in the audience all along. McGillicutty was stooped, had a bad limp, and his hat was pulled well down over his eyes. No wonder I had not recognized him in the audience. He was climbing into a hack less than a block away.

I started to go after him. "No need to run after him. He lives at the Marshall Hotel at State and Van Buren." My sallow-faced friend spoke from the corner of his mouth and scuttled away before I could thank him.

Dr. Bell was still lecturing, and it would not hurt to delay my meeting with Dr. McGillicutty, so I returned and watched while Dr. Murphy neatly sewed up the incisions in poor Fogarty and Dr. Bell lectured on glands. He is as knowledgeable on the subject as anyone in the world, but very little is really known about them.

The amphitheatre was very warm and the session bogged down in a discussion of philosophy and even Darwin's theory. I found myself drifting off to sleep.

16 November, 1878

My day was filled with more lectures and dissections, so I was not free until late in the day. In Chicago, as in Edinburgh, dusk comes early, especially on those overcast days with a foreboding of snow. The Harrison Street Omnibus took me to State Street which was only a short walk to Van Buren.

The streets were filled with disreputable men, poorly dressed women, and raggedy lads. Many carried unlit torches, and there was an air of excitement in the crowd. I hurried on, ignoring the moving swarm of people, and kept a hand on my wallet. The Marshall Hotel was a hastily slapped-together structure next to a gambling parlor and across the street from an empty lot filled with rubbish.

I shivered against the wind, and a knot of cold fear clutched the center of my chest. I started to freeze and then stopped myself. What was I doing? Did I have the nerve to do this? Was it foolhardy to pursue a criminal alone? Was I merely trying to prove my worth to myself and Dr. Bell?

I hesitated, but pressed forward into the shabby, dark lobby where a clerk directed me to the corner room overlooking State Street. "Who is there?" The gruff question came in answer to my knock on the door.

"My name is Doyle, assistant to Dr. Joseph Bell."

I was not sure how he would respond. "The door is open. Enter." The voice had a strange tone, but was not unpleasant.

As soon as I walked in I backed away—repulsed by the overpowering odor of decay—and covered my face with a handkerchief. By the light of a single candle stuck in an old wine bottle I made out a bed, table, and a chair. Then, as my eyes adjusted, I saw movement under a pile of blankets on the bed. The dim figure gradually sat up and swung his legs off the side of the bed.

"Mr. Doyle, you have been looking for me?"

The voice had a peculiar resonance, and, as the figure gradually came into the candle's light, I saw a face disfigured by deep crevices, flat red patches, and a sunken nose. It was nothing like the photograph of Dr. McGillicutty. Was this an imposter to throw me off the scent? Maybe he had syphilis.

"Um, are you . . . Are you Doctor McGillicutty?" I stammered.

"None other."

"But, you don't look like your pictures."

"Mr. Doyle, you have followed me from the hospital, aye? I was there and saw you. I had to witness the post-mortem examination of poor Fogarty. He was one of my patients, you know?"

I took a step forward, but he held up his hand and motioned for me to come no closer. The hand was misshapen and the tips of the fingers ulcerated.

"Have they taught you about leprosy at Edinburgh?"

I recoiled in panic. "There might have been a lecture, but I don't remember."

His laugh was hollow and mournful. "Study my face and hands."

"But, I thought leprosy was only in the tropics."

"You are seeing the revenge of a monkey. I caught the disease from an experimental animal."

"What sort of experiments?"

"I worked on glandular extracts, looking for a cure for poor unfortunates like Fogarty."

"Then, you <u>are</u> the one. You murder men for their thyroid glands."

"No, no, no... Please, look at these hands. I have not operated for a long while." He waved his misshapen hands for me to inspect, although from a distance. I realized he was right. There was no way he could have performed delicate surgery with such deformed digits.

"But, you know about glandular extracts and—"

"Yes. My experiments with monkeys demonstrated that extracts of fresh tissue reversed the effects of total thyroidectomy. Sadly, I had to work on live, awake animals because, otherwise, anaesthetics reduced the potency of the glandular extracts I needed."

"And you used curare to prevent the animals from moving while you were experimenting on them?"

"Exactly. Until, one day, I administered too low a dose of curare to a poor creature, and the monkey awoke in mid-operation and bit me. The damn animal infected me with leprosy."

"Sir, I believe that someone knows of your work and is killing humans to obtain the thyroid."

"You are correct. I suspect it is one of my former associates. Doyle, if you can stand the sight of my poor broken body, I would be willing to share all I know with you."

"Yes, Doctor, should we talk here or . . ."

"I haven't had a morsel of food all day. Let's go out and get something to eat. You know, your mentor, Dr. Bell may be the only surgeon in the world who can truly understand my work."

My heart went out to the wretched man. I wondered what it was like to have a horrible, incurable disease and feel death hovering over you. I shivered again and felt a premonition of ominous things to come.

The poor man pulled on gloves and turned the brim of his hat down over his face. Together, we exited his tiny room. As we made our way down the street to his favourite restaurant I made out a band of armed men lurking in the area just past the hotel. As if in a bad dream, I watched as they raised their weapons and took aim. *Dear God. Is this the end?* I dove into the shadows just as shots rang out. I was unscathed. Dr. McGillicutty was not so lucky. A fusillade of bullets struck him down.

Instinctively, I crawled to his aid, barely avoiding injury myself when a slug tore through the sleeve of my heavy coat. McGillicutty had bloody holes in his chest. The sound of gunfire was suddenly drowned out by shouts and the clip-clop of horses on the pavement.

Was it a diversion to mask the murder? The night was lit by hundreds of blazing torches carried by demonstrators shouting for justice and higher wages. I huddled with McGillicutty on the sidewalk as a phalanx of mounted men dressed in white hoods and robes marched by, followed by men and lads shouting and carrying banners denouncing capitalism. All of them were oblivious to poor Dr. McGillicutty.

I held two fingers against Dr. McGillicutty's neck. There was no pulse. He was beyond help. Knowing it was too late for him, I escaped the raucous hubbub through an alley while I still could.

I could still hear the shouts and gunfire behind me as I crept between buildings until I was away from the demonstration. When I was finally in the clear, I broke into a dead run to Mr. Duncan's mansion.

In order to avoid disturbing anyone, I decided to go around the back and through the servant's entrance into the kitchen.

By this time it was so late, and I was able to sneak through the entire house and make my way to my room without being spotted.

Once I arrived in my quarters I was so exhausted that I was asleep before I could take off all my clothes.

17 November, 1878

I slept almost till noon and then spent most of the afternoon walking the streets of Chicago, thinking through last night's events. When night fell, I returned to Mr. Duncan's house where many fine carriages lined the front entrance to the mansion. As I walked by the great living room I stopped and listened to agitated conversation. ". . . What business do Southerners have up here?"

"I attribute it to all those bastard foreign anarchists."

"Yes, and don't forget the damn socialists."

I paused long enough to recognize the voice of Allan Pinkerton. "Gentlemen, my men will put down this riot and shoot the instigators."

"That's all well and good, but what is the Klan doing in Chicago?" another voice asked.

Pinkerton's voice rose. "Gentlemen, please, let me finish. There appears to be a group of Southerners who are attempting to ally themselves with local union organizers to disrupt our nation."

There was a stunned silence. "How, in the name of God could that happen?" asked a gentleman with a fevered voice.

Pinkerton went on. "Gentlemen, yesterday one hundred Gatling guns and a thousand new Winchester repeating rifles were stolen from the armory. I fear that they will be used to arm troops in the South or to foment uprisings among disgruntled workingmen right here in this fair city. Either way, it is not good."

I had heard enough and crept up the stairs. I was surprised to find the door to Dr. Bell's room wide open. "Doyle, please join me for a bit of supper."

I set to work on smoked turkey, a bit of pork roast, preserved strawberries, tea, and bread smeared with butter. Dr. Bell sipped Mr. Duncan's fine malt whisky and gazed into the blazing fire. "The Americans seem to have themselves a bit of a crisis," said he. "But, enough about them, what have you been up to, my lad?"

I had to make a clean breast of it and confessed that I had left the hospital to pursue the investigation. Dr. Bell humphed and harrumphed as I told him of my encounter with Dr. McGillicutty. The whole while he sat with his fingers laced over his chest, looking deeply into the flames. When I came to the part about the doctor's leprosy, he shook his head. "Sad, so sad."

When I finished my dismal story, he became alert and had that glint in his eye that I knew so well. "Damn it, Doyle, do you realize that your meddling may have caused that poor man's death?"

"I don't think . . . How could—"

"Who knew you were meeting with him and that you were involved with the investigation?"

"I am so sorry." I hung my head and wished that I had never come to America. "I didn't . . . Well, I never meant to cause him harm."

"Just answer my question."

"The father of the little girl with croup knew I wanted to meet Dr. McGillicutty. He seemed to be an honest workingman."

"Who else?"

"Well, there were many other people in the tavern that day."

"So, there were others who could have overheard your conversation with Fogarty?"

"Yes, and oh, there was that woman."

"That woman?"

"The one you are fond of who attends the clinic."

"I am not *fond* of her. She is a student of the medical arts. Nothing more and nothing less."

"She left the post-mortem early and may have overheard my conversation with the girl's father."

"Hmm . . . Now, Doyle, I regret to say this, but do you realize that your meddling may have also bungled our entire investigation?"

I felt awful. "I am so sorry, sir. Is there anything I can say or do—"

"On the other hand, you may have turned up an important clue. Fogarty was murdered to prevent him from revealing Dr. McGillicutty's location and some unknown person or persons killed the doctor to prevent him from discussing his work and his comrades with you."

I was overcome by guilt and remorse at my folly and was scarcely listening. He squeezed my arm to bring me out of my guilty funk.

"Doyle, please lad, listen to me. What were McGillicutty's exact words? Are you certain he said comrades instead of colleagues or classmates?"

"I think he said comrade. What difference does it make, sir?"

"My lad, have you learned nothing on this trip? You must not only learn to observe diligently, but to listen carefully and analyze the meaning of each word. Obviously the word colleague refers to a close associate, such as a physician's partner. The word comrade, on the other hand, is often applied to one's friends in a military outfit."

"Heavens above. That reminds me." I hastily consulted my notes. "Dr. McGillicutty was a surgeon in the Confederate Army."

"Exactly, lad, and a Confederate bayonet killed Fogarty . . . Yet I cannot connect his statement about going south and a red house with anything concrete related to these murders."

"What about those three words scrawled in blood by Fogarty? Did you discover their meaning?"

"Mrs. O'Flynn confirmed that *cinnte faoi ghlas is* Gaelic and means 'sure lock.' "

"Sure lock . . . That could be the name of a type of lock box or a safe." I said.

"Aye, most likely. Do you think Fogarty may have been directing you to a specific safe that contained some item of great value?" Dr. Bell asked.

There was a gentle knock on the door.

"Who is there?" Dr. Bell asked.

"Rufus."

"Come in, please."

Rufus stumbled into the room and stood before us, speechless. He trembled and twisted his cap in his hands.

"Rufus snap out of it, man. What the devil is wrong?" Dr. Bell asked.

"They's coming after all us freedmen. To make us slaves again. I gots to go back to the *Devonia*. Get clear out of this country."

"Mr. Freeman, please calm down. Have a drink to settle your nerves."

Dr. Bell filled a crystal glass with several fingers of malt whisky. Rufus gulped it all down in one swallow.

"President Lincoln freed the slaves and the Thirteenth Amendment assured their freedom. You have nothing to worry about," said Dr. Bell.

"They killed poor Mr. Lincoln and those ghosts marchin' in the street gonna tear up that 'mancipation proclamation. My lady friend's a housekeeper at the hotel and she told me that she was brushin' a man's suit when she seen them ghost clothes."

"Ghost clothes?"

"Yes sir. White hoods, long white robes. He had a set in the closet just like they was wearing on the street."

"Who is this man?"

"Captain Andrew Spencer. He was in the rebel army and rode with General Forrest. He got his right hand blowed off at the battle of Corinth and turned plumb mean."

"Did he stay in the rebel army?"

"Yes, sir. The doctors fixed a hook on his right arm so he could grab things. He kilt prisoners at Fort Pillow after they surrendered. Those poor bluecoats knelt down and begged for mercy, but he kilt them in cold blood. They called him Captain Hook."

"Can you describe his hook?"

"It was made out of iron, curved like this and sharp at the end." Rufus bent his finger in the shape of a half circle.

"Doyle, let me see that fragment from Fogarty's skull."

I handed him the sharp metallic sliver. Dr. Bell drew the lamp closer, placed the fragment on a slip of paper. He minutely studied the bit of metal with a magnifying glass. I fidgeted and wondered why a small bit of metal was so interesting or important. "Doyle, tell me what am I doing and why."

"Um . . . Ah, well, you are trying to determine if that metal is iron or steel or—"

"No, Doyle. Sometimes you appear rather clever. But, then, there are other times when you seem a bit dense."

"Sorry, sir."

"Shush. Please sit in that chair and imagine what you would do if I attempted to drive a knife into your mouth."

"I would clench my teeth and resist, moving my head from side to side."

"Exactly. And, unless it was tightly held as the knife was thrust in, your head would move back. As a result, there would not be enough force to penetrate the vertebra."

Dr. Bell then clasped the back of my head with his left hand and drove an imaginary knife into my mouth.

"See. Most likely, the assailant drove the point of an instrument into the back of poor Fogarty's skull and held it, while, with his left hand, he drove the bayonet from left to right into the vertebra."

"Captain Hook, or should I say Captain Spencer, is most definitely our man," I said.

"Not so fast, my laddie. Have I not taught you to be wary of jumping to false conclusions?"

I hung my head in shame. "Aye, sir."

"Mr. Freeman, what do you know about the people in these white robes?"

"They's the ghosts of soldiers who got killed in the war. They ride at night and burn crosses and hang poor Negroes that ain't done nothin' wrong. They's used to be found only down South, but now they's haunting the night right here in Chicago."

"Mr. Freeman, my friend, let me assure you there is no such thing as ghosts. These people garbed all in white are flesh and blood, just like you or me. Now, please, if you will, give me a moment to think."

Dr. Bell stretched his legs to the fire and for several minutes was lost in thought.

After what was probably no more than five minutes Bell sprang up out of his chair and paced the floor. "Mr. Freeman, do you know the Captain's room number at the hotel?"

"I can find out."

"Doyle, to-morrow, go into town and purchase a half-pound of gunpowder and two ounces of sulphur. Mr. Freeman, secure a porter's uniform for yourself. And to-night, both of you, please get a good night's sleep. There's a good deal of work to be done."

Rufus and I nodded in agreement. "Yes, sir."

"Excellent... Gentlemen, the game is afoot."

18 November, 1878

America is a strange county. It is a nation so full of energy and in such a rush to be a world leader, yet still so backward. For example, Americans have the quaint idea that sulphur is a sovereign remedy for many ills including pains, fevers, and upset stomachs. I found sulphur in a chemist shop among other patent remedies. "Take a pinch of the sulphur in a tablespoon full of molasses. You will be set right in no time," the chemist advised.

He, then, kindly directed me to a store that sold gunpowder and a variety of firearms. I could not ignore the irony of visiting a gun shop in order to cure one's ills . . .

I purchased the gunpowder. While paying the bill, I looked longingly at the Winchester rifles, Colt six-shooters, and a wide variety of pistols, daggers, holsters, and all the equipment necessary to subdue wild animals, Indians, and all the other deadly dangers lurking in the wilds of the American continent.

After my recent narrow escapes I was determined to purchase a weapon to defend myself. The .45 calibre Colt revolver really took my fancy, but I settled on an easily concealed two-shot .32 calibre Remington Derringer.

"If you are concerned about personal protection, may I also recommend this item?" the clerk asked. It was a thin, very sharp stiletto about five inches long that would fit into a sheathed strapped to one's leg or forearm. It would be instantly available in case of an attack. I thought back to my assailant on the *Devonia* and could not resist. I walked out of the store with the stiletto in a sheath, firmly strapped just above my right ankle under my wool stocking. With a gun and a knife, I felt like the hero, Hawkeye, in my favourite American adventure book, *The Last of the Mohicans*. For the first time since arriving in Chicago, I felt safe.

The rest of the day, I worked in the laboratory with Carl Lindborg. We dissected the intricate tendons and nerves in the hand of our cadaver. Carl was such a good fellow that, after swearing him to secrecy, I told him of my adventures with Fogarty and Dr. McGillicutty.

"Artie, these are violent times here in America. Everything might be quaint and safe in good old Edinburgh, but here we're in the grips of a terrible financial recession. Why do you think I left our farm in Wisconsin? Ever since I arrived here in Chicago, there have been strikes and killings over wages and worker's rights. It's worse down South, where people are boiling over with resentment against the carpetbaggers and President Hayes who they think stole the last election." Carl spoke with the fervor of the downtrodden. "Still, for the sake of Dr. McGillicutty, shouldn't I investigate fur—"

"As your friend, I beg you to be careful . . . With that said, there is nothing I like more than a grand adventure. If you want to be foolhardy and get to the root of these murders, I am the man to go with you and keep you safe."

Later, Dr. Bell brooded over Carl's words but made no comment. Finally, he looked at me. "The authorities are unable to solve these murders. The Pinkerton detectives scoff at our methods. A less stubborn man would quit right now, but I owe it to my old friend, Angus, to continue our investigations. I trust we shall get to the bottom of this mystery over the course of this very evening."

"But, how?"

"Well, dear laddie, all we have to do is follow my plan."

A few hours later, Carl and I were wearing our very best suits and smoking fine cigars as we strolled into the lobby of the Tremont Hotel. We looked like two fine young dandies out for drinks, dinner, and a night on the town. We were not alone. Stylish ladies and gentlemen were scattered here and there, chatting on stuffed leather chairs. Others were drifting in and out of the dining room. We finally settled into a pair of chairs next to a low table in a corner not far from the grand open staircase.

I placed a folded newspaper beneath the table. Hidden inside was a rolled-up sheet of paper holding a small quantity of gunpowder. I had twisted each end of the paper to contain the powder as well as to work as a sort of fuse. When Rufus, dressed in a porter's uniform, raised his hand, I applied my cigar to the twisted end. When it began to 'sizzle,' Carl and I casually strolled towards the entrance.

Just as Dr. Bell predicted, exactly ten seconds later there was a loud *whoosh*, flying sparks, flames, and a dense cloud of yellow, sulphurous smoke. People ran to and fro, coughing, gagging, screaming, covering their faces with handkerchiefs, and making for the exits.

Almost immediately, a bell clanged and more guests swarmed down the main staircase. Rufus dashed through the smoke and stamped out the flames, but the sulphur continued to smolder.

The smoke cleared, but the pandemonium continued. I noticed a petite lady hurrying down the staircase. Even though her face was covered, there was no mistaking the elegant Emilie Droussard on the arm of a ramrod-straight gentleman wearing a grey suit and gloves.

Porters and clerks scurried about, attempting to restore order. Carl and I waited for a full ten minutes, as instructed, but Dr. Bell did not appear. After a few more minutes of waiting for him Carl and I went from perplexed to deeply worried.

Next thing we knew, as a few guests were venturing back up the grand staircase, Rufus and a girl in a maid's uniform ran up to us. Rufus could barely get out the words, "They killed him!"

"Who?" I asked.

"Dr. Bell!"

Great heavens! We ran upstairs and found him lying, absolutely still, in a pool of blood in the corridor outside the open door to room 203.

There was a long gash on the side of his face. With each faint heartbeat more blood pumped out onto the oriental rug in the hallway. Dr. Bell was still alive, but barely. I should have reacted, but, for all my training, I trembled. Dr. Bell, who usually told me what to do, was unconscious and bleeding. Carl staunched the bleeding with a folded handkerchief pressed against his scalp. I looked into Carl's calm face and saw that he was a natural physician, while I—I was the son of a drunk and a dreamer.

"Look at me! Snap out of it, Artie, for God's sake, we must get him out of here."

I snapped out of my trance. "My name is Arthur, can't you learn?"

"Never mind. We need to get him to Mr. Duncan's house right now or he could die. Our safest route is down the servant's stairs and through the kitchen out to the alley. Follow me."

I held pressure on the wound while he and Rufus carried the doctor. As we walked through the kitchen we kept our heads down and tried to ignore the firemen and police who were restoring order. And then, I felt a hand on my shoulder.

I froze and looked up into the eyes of a burly, red-faced Chicago policeman. "Where you two going so fast? Is that man alive?"

Carl spoke up. "We are medical students assisting an injured guest, sir. This man is badly injured. We are taking him to the County Hospital."

The policeman seemed satisfied with Carl's response. We kept moving. During the journey to Mr. Duncan's house, Dr. Bell moaned in pain and appeared to gain consciousness.

Carl and Rufus put the doctor to bed. The deep laceration did not reach down to the skull and appeared to be due to a glancing blow. The profuse bleeding subsided to a slow trickle after I dressed the gash with carbolic gauze and applied a large pressure bandage.

I was beside myself. Would Dr. Bell live through the night? Had I failed him? Would he be in this horrible condition if not for me? If I had dressed the wound poorly and it got infected, I could never live with myself.

I wanted to stay by Dr. Bell all night, but there was nothing left to do. Rufus and Carl forced me to go back to my room to get some sleep. I wrote out the day's events and even prayed for Dr. Bell . . .

19 November, 1878

When I awoke in the morning, I went straight to Dr. Bell's room and knocked on his door. There was no answer. My heart sank: was he dead?

Then, I heard his voice from the kitchen. There he was, healthy enough to sip at Mrs. O'Flynn's homemade chicken soup. It looked scrumptious, and I joined him for a bowl.

The bandage was clean and his skin was no longer deathly white. At noon, after he had insisted upon eating a bowl of Scottish oatmeal, he was sufficiently recovered to relate a rather disconnected, garbled version of his adventure.

"When the fire alarm sounded, I dashed up the servant's staircase to the second floor undetected. Rufus's lady friend provided a key for me to enter Captain Spencer's room. Just as Rufus said, there was a grey officer's uniform with the insignia of a major general in the closet. My memory is still clouded, but I think there was a white hooded robe and several articles of women's clothing."

Dr. Bell's head drooped on the pillow for a long minute, and he covered his eyes with both hands. "If only I could remember more specifics," said he.

"Were there any documents?" I asked.

"Aye . . . Good. Press me, my dear Doyle . . . Help me clarify my thoughts."

"Professor, what did the documents say?"

"I remember . . . A list of names . . . Jefferson Davis . . . Wade Hampton . . . It seems to me that the name Beecher was on the list . . . There were other names, but I just can't remember."

"Did you see Spencer's iron hook appendage?"

"No, but the door to the adjacent room was ajar. I remember now. There was a table with retorts, mortar and pestle, various sized bottles and test tubes, and syringes with needles."

"Chemical apparatus and equipment for medical experiments?"

"Aye, exactly. But, at that very moment, I was struck from behind and was barely able to stagger into the corridor before collapsing and losing consciousness."

"Did you see your assailants?"

"I sensed that there were two large men."

For a moment, Dr. Bell's eyes took on their familiar keen twinkle. "Now, my dear Doyle, everything I've taught you about observing the world comes into play. Tell me. It is vitally important. Did you see anyone come down the stairs?" he asked.

"Well, sir, let's see . . ." I paused. "Carl and I were so nervous about setting off the charge of gunpowder that I didn't notice. "There were dozens of people milling about, making for the exits."

"Think hard."

"Ah, yes. There was a man dressed in a grey suit, walking rather stiffly. I am certain Emilie Droussard was at his side. I may have also seen them together the morning we had breakfast at the hotel."

"Was there anything unusual about his right hand?"

"He wore gloves."

"Was the woman holding his right or left arm?"

"I think she was on his right side, holding his right arm."

"Did that strike you as unusual?"

"No."

"Now, Doyle, a man usually offers his left arm to a lady, so his dominant right hand is free."

I saw the trend of his thought. "Then, if his right hand was useless, he would offer his right arm to the lady."

"Exactly. Captain Spencer or, as he is called, 'Captain Hook', was wearing an imitation hand, covered with a glove. But, why would he be with Emilie? Hmm . . ."

20 November, 1878

Dr. Bell has spent a good deal of time in his bedroom staring off into space, or in the library huddled with Angus Duncan.

Meanwhile, I have been attempting to keep up with my medical studies by attending lectures and assisting in the anatomy laboratory. This morning, Dr. Bell requested that I attend a meeting with Allan Pinkerton and Mr. Duncan.

Dr. Bell sat up in bed with his hands folded and explained the purpose of the meeting. "Doyle, Mr. Pinkerton has ascertained that our suspects have absconded from the hotel, leaving no clues as to their destination. Further investigation has revealed the identities of the most recent victims. They were newly recruited Pinkerton detectives assigned to Mr. Duncan's Chicago, St. Louis and New Orleans's railway. However, none of them have ever reported for work."

I helped Bell walk down to the great drawing room where Allan Pinkerton and Mr. Duncan were having tea.

"These poor devils were murdered to prevent their work in protecting the railways." Pinkerton spoke with a great air of superiority.

"But . . ." I tried to introduce my thoughts. He rose and cut me off with a wave of his hand.

"Listen to me, lad. I know about these things, and their deaths have nothing to do with your ridiculous theory of organ removal."

"But, we have absolute evidence in one case that the thyroid gland was removed, and the equipment Dr. Bell found could very well have been used to prepare a glandular extract from the thyroid." My Irish was up. The man was a pompous ass.

Mr. Pinkerton ignored my outburst and spread a map of the United States on the desk. He tapped the route of the railway from Chicago to New Orleans. "Whoever controls this railroad can move troops to Chicago and control the western half of the country. It is then only one day to transport a Southern army, augmented by communists and Molly Maguire's, to seize Pittsburgh and other major industrial cities. The Federal Army is spread thin attempting to control Indians. So, if the rebels choose to attack, there is actually very little we could do to stop the South from taking over the country and restoring slavery."

"Does that explain the presence of Captain Spencer in Chicago?" I asked.

"Young man, that is none of your business."

"Allan, you are mistaken. Mr. Doyle has risked his life to unravel this mystery. It is very much his business." Angus Duncan's reply was somewhat testy. I was happy for his support.

"But, he is a foreigner and only a student," Pinkerton retorted.

"I trust him and you must, too, sir." There was a pregnant pause as both men stared at each other and then looked at Bell . . .

Finally, Pinkerton nodded. "Oh, very well. After the Civil War the federal authorities charged Captain Spencer with murder for killing soldiers after they surrendered. He escaped to Mexico and joined Maximillian's army, then went to Venezuela where he made his fortune in gold mines. Sadly, the Hayes administration has pardoned all war criminals. He has returned, is dangerous, and is determined to restore the Confederacy."

"Who is Emilie Droussard?" I asked.

"All we really know is that after her husband was killed at Vicksburg she became a Confederate spy," Pinkerton answered.

There was a pause in the conversation until Dr. Bell commented. "Aye, Doyle, our enemies are quite brilliant. If we are to stop these butchers and survive this investigation, I daresay we must be even more clever . . ."

22 November, 1878

Dr. Bell disappeared yesterday. When I saw him this morning, there were subtle changes in his appearance. His cheeks were drawn, and lines had appeared in his face. Even his hair was darker and unruly. I looked more closely. "Doctor Bell, are you still not well?"

"Why do you ask, lad?"

"Well, as you have taught me, I'm trying to make subtle observations. For example, it seems to me that in just two days your hair has changed from pure white to a dull grey-brown."

"Bravo, my dear Doyle. Bravo. It appears as if all my efforts in training you have not been in vain, after all." He flung down a copy of *The Chicago Tribune*. "Read this aloud, laddie."

Bell watched me read with a twinkle in his eye. "Edinburgh surgeon, Dr. Joseph Bell, has been visiting our city and is reported to be seriously ill and near death. If his health improves, he will return to Scotland."

"This makes no sense. Why would they write this?"

"Doyle, are you familiar with *Didelphis Virginiana*?"

"Excuse me?"

"You might be more familiar with this creature by its common name—the Virginia opossum. When this creature senses danger, he curls into a ball and feigns death."

I thought for a moment and then smiled. "And you intend to play that same game to lure our opponents out into the open."

"Astute, my lad. Quite astute. Maybe my lessons are finally paying off."

Another of Bell's peculiarities is the daily reading of newspapers from all different states in America. As he reads one paper after another, he discards them into a stack. I have read in the discarded papers about such things as Nez Perce Indians fleeing through Montana to Canada, Texans fighting over the Mexican border, and Irish miners being hung in Pennsylvania.

So, then, I was not at all surprised when he handed over a copy of *The Memphis Daily Appeal.* "They have struck again, Doyle. Look."

He pointed to an article on the third page which mentioned a young man collapsing on the street and his body immediately being removed. And then he pointed to a story on the back page which announced a series of sermons by the Reverend Henry Ward Beecher and the Scots minister, the Reverend James Balfour, on the subjects of slavery and social Darwinism.

"What do you propose we do about it?" I asked.

"I must go there, but in disguise. I owe it to my old friend, Angus, to see this through. He has paid a hefty fee to get us here and has entrusted us with solving this enigma . . . But, my dear Doyle, you are under no obligation to continue with what will be a dangerous mission. Feel free to return home to your mother."

"Sir, I may be many things, but a craven lad who runs home to his mother, I am not. And, by and by, I have always wanted to visit Memphis in Tennessee, as well."

"An epidemic of yellow fever has been raging through that fair city since August. Thousands have already died."

"That does not change my mind."

He chuckled. "I expected you would say that . . . And you must know, if you go, Doyle, your life will be in danger and you will have to pose as a Pinkerton man."

"A Pinkerton?"

"You will be disguised and will need a sturdy companion. You will be well paid, and there might be a reward if this case has a satisfactory outcome."

"I know the perfect bloke."

"Your mate, Mr. Lindborg, I presume?"

"Why, of course."

"It is agreed then. Allan Pinkerton will prepare two sets of papers for you and Mr. Lindborg. The first will establish you as medical volunteers to assist with the yellow fever epidemic, and the second set will identify you as special security agents for the Illinois Central Railroad."

Carl was eager for the adventure, and, together, we went to the Pinkerton Detective Agency. It was located in an imposing three-story building with a huge sign along the second story which read 'THE EYE THAT NEVER SLEEPS'.

When we entered the building, a clerk conducted us to the office of the general superintendent where we signed the payroll and obtained our two sets of papers. The pay was six dollars a day, and our task was to 'keep an eye on things.' Under no circumstances were we to partake of hard liquor or behave in any way that would dishonour the agency.

On our return, Dr. Bell gave us further instructions. "When you arrive in Memphis, stay at the Peabody Hotel and volunteer to aid the sick. At night, spend time in the saloons, pretend to be intoxicated, and brag about being security officers for the railroad."

"For six dollars a day I can do that," said Carl.

"Wait, sir, is that all?" I asked.

Dr. Bell sighed, "Above all, always stay close. Never let each other out of your sight and follow one another when you are on the streets. The poison curare primarily affects skeletal muscles. If you ever feel a pinprick, it may be a poisonous needle. You must concentrate on nothing else, but breathing with your diaphragm. That is less affected by the poison."

"I'm sorry, sir, but what does being a Pinkerton have to do with curare and practicing breathing?"

"Well, dear laddie, you and Carl will be bait for the killers. I would do it myself if I was younger, but alas . . ."

"You mean, we may be in danger from the killers who use curare?"

"Aye, this is a deadly game. Lad, you may back out if you wish."

"No, I am armed and with Carl. We will have no fear of those ruffians."

I spoke with great bravado, but with an undercurrent of fear. And then, despite my determination to put Rebecca out of mind, I wondered about whether she was with the Reverend Balfour in Memphis and if I might see her again.

23 November, 1878

I did not sleep well last night and dreamed about poison and ghastly medical experiments. I greatly admired Dr. Bell's deductive talents, but did his cognitive faculties overshadow common sense and his ability to empathize with the plight of others?

The idea of posing as Pinkertons smacked of lunacy and sheer madness. Several times in the wee hours of the morning, I vowed I would march right over to his room and tell him to get another poor sod to serve as his live bait.

In the end, it was clear we were committed. Both Carl and I needed the money. I am already in too deep and must not let down Doctor Bell or Carl.

Rufus came early to help pack. "Mr. Arthur, those folks down south don't take to strangers from the North. Don't you trust nobody and be careful."

"I shall."

"I want to go with you."

"No, Rufus. You stay with Dr. Bell."

Rufus bobbed his woolly head. "Guess you is right. I'll stick with the doctor, but they's one white man in Memphis you can trust."

"Who?"

"Mr. Josiah Burk on Second Street."

He then took a common pin out of his wallet and a pinch of black soot wrapped in a scrap of paper. "Hold out your wrist." He dipped the pin in the soot and pricked the inside of my wrist, leaving an almost microscopic black dot. "Show him this mark. He helped slaves escape to the North."

I finished writing these bits of conversation and my sad ruminations. I then gave this diary to Doctor Bell with a folded note that said, "Sir, if we don't return, please give this to my mother."

An hour later, Carl and I climbed aboard the crowded smoking car of the *St. Louis Flyer*. It was ten o'clock in the morning as we rattled through Central Illinois. I was tired and morose at leaving Dr. Bell and the dangers that may lie ahead. Carl was jubilant.

"Carl, how can you be so calm?"

Carl puffed on his El Perfecto cigar and smiled. "In just ten days on this job, I am gonna earn sixty dollars. My pa don't see that much money for a year of hard work. It will save our family's farm and pay for Rush Medical School next year."

"That's all well and good, but you won't be able to collect your sixty dollars if you're <u>DEAD</u>!"

"Doyle, you Scottish worry-wart! We'll be fine . . ."

I began to settle down and watch the never-ending prairie, fields of corn, and sluggish rivers. Carl never stopped talking, puffing his El Perfecto cigar, and pointing out landmarks. He had a natural understanding of the land and botany. He knew the names of the rivers Kankakee and Illinois, and recognized the small towns. Later in the journey, the land was bleak and flat compared to the braes of Scotland. I felt a pang of homesickness and had images of a girl with red hair in the heather.

24 November, 1878

(I am writing this from memory since I did not have my journal for several days)

It took all day to get to East St. Louis where the train cars were loaded on a ferry boat that crossed the Mississippi River. We pulled into the Relay Depot in St. Louis just after four o'clock in the morning, pretty well covered with grit and soot and hungry as bear cubs. In the depot we had fried egg sandwiches and about the worst cup of coffee I ever tasted.

Our old train needed work, so we got on a new one bound for Memphis. Although, the word *new* probably should not be used since the locomotive had an old pokey engine . . . The train had a coal car, a luggage car, and three passenger cars. One was a smoker, but it was filled. We had to get on the second-class carriage where there were only a few empty seats. I remembered Doctor Bell's last admonition, "Boys, don't get separated," but there was nothing to do. I sat next to a grizzled, bearded old farmer, and Carl found a spot a few seats forward.

The talkative farmer took a chaw of tobacco. "We ain't got nothing to worry about on this train, no sir. There's Pinkertons on board, you know, but they's probably dressed like ordinary folks," said he.

I gulped. If he only knew. "Really? Um, eh . . . Why would you think there are Pinkertons on board today?"

"To protect all that cotton money. Why else?"

"Cotton money?" I asked.

"Why, every year, bankers up North send a safe full of money to Memphis to buy cotton. And when they do, they always hire extra guards."

I was beginning to feel uncomfortable. No one said anything about guarding a safe full of money . . . And, speaking of safes, could this farmer sitting next to me be making a reference to Fogarty's *sure lock* safe?

I must have looked nervous because the farmer offered a bottle of whisky. I overcame my scruples and glugged a healthy swallow. It was rotten homemade stuff, not like smooth malt Scotch whisky.

I tried to relax by looking out the window. We were south of St. Louis. The train wound through hills and over streams and rivers on rickety bridges. I was keeping my eyes peeled for Indians when we entered a dense forest that was what I always imagined America would look like. There were occasional patches of corn and shacks, but, unfortunately, no red men.

When the train stopped at a village, I decided to get out and stretch my legs. I looked around. The whole town seemed to be nothing more than a general store, a blacksmith shop, and a few run-down log cabins.

The grizzled old farmer had followed. "Ain't nothing but poor folks here. The damn Yankees took everything we had. 'Bout time we drove the dang carpetbaggers back up North where they belong," he said, and spit a stream of tobacco juice.

"Were folks hereabouts sympathetic with the Confederates?" I asked.

"You're damn right we were. I reckon things get any worse, we're gonna raise us another rebel force."

The train whistle blew. We boarded and took our seats. Carl was sound asleep a few rows away.

The train lurched and swayed on the curves at thirty or forty miles an hour until we came to a hill and down a long curve to a valley. The train was not going more than ten miles an hour between a cliff and a small river. All of a sudden, the air brakes screeched and the train crashed to a stop.

Our carriage shuddered and stayed upright, but the engine and the coal car slipped off the rails and went into a ditch. Folks in our carriage were jostled and shook. I slammed into the seat in front and the farmer fell into the aisle, but no one was badly hurt.

I looked out the window and saw men on horseback riding down from the hill, whooping and hollering and swearing something awful. They fired at the train. One shot shattered a window in our car. Suddenly, an ear-piercing *BOOM!* came from the baggage car up ahead. Pieces of train flew in the air then rained down to earth. The bandits continued shooting guns and whooping.

"Are those wild Indians?" I asked.

"Nah, more likely to be them James boys. They blew the safe. Good for them."

Women screamed and children cried. Everyone tried to hide their valuables. I checked my little pistol and felt for the stiletto. Should I make a brave stand and take out one of the bandits? Pretty soon, two men carrying large revolvers, their faces covered with masks, came into the carriage. One fellow was tall, skinny, and sandy-haired, and the other was big-bellied and wore a black, broad-brimmed hat.

The tall, skinny fellow pulled down his scarf to reveal whiskers and a snub nose. "You folks just stay still, put your hands up, and no one'll get hurt."

He held his revolver to the conductor's head and pulled back the hammer.

"Show me them Pinkertons."

"Yes, sir, Mr. James." The conductor pointed first at Carl and then at me. I tried to pull the .32 Derringer from my coat pocket, but the old farmer grabbed my arm. "Put that damn pea shooter away before you get us all killed."

"But—"

"Shush your mouth. That there fellow is Jesse James."

James and his partner came down the aisle, smiling and joking as if they were having the best time in the world. The dark-haired, fat gent carried an open feed sack. He stopped before a rather plain-looking woman and smiled as if she was a real looker. "Please, ma'am, put your money and jewelry in the bag."

Jesse James was polite as he could be to the passengers, but he turned mean and surly when he stopped at my seat. "So, this is one of those damn Pinkerton fellas? I oughta blow off your damn head!"

I hunkered down and tried to look innocent. Carl, blazing with his hot temper, rose to his full height and stared at Jesse James. "The name's Carl Lindborg and I'll lick you and your whole gang."

Jesse smiled. "You can start by licking my ass," he answered.

James and his gang howled with peals of laughter. Jesse walked over to Carl and poked his revolver into Carl's ribs. "This here Colt can blow a hole right through your gut. Say one more word and you are dead meat."

I threw aside caution. "Mr. James, please don't shoot! He likes to talk tough, but we aren't Pinkertons. We're both medical students going to Memphis to help with the yellow fever victims."

James jammed his big Colt revolver into my ribs. "Your accent sounds like that blowhard Pinkerton."

"Aye, I'm Irish, but grew up in Scotland and proud of it."

"Pinkerton can't get men no more, so he gets boys to do his dirty work, eh?"

"Lemme kill 'em, boss." The fat gunslinger begged.

"Nah, they might come in handy later." He trained the revolver first on me, then on Carl. He pulled back the hammer and squeezed the trigger. I figured Carl was a goner, but the revolver made a harmless click. Carl went pale as a sheet. Jesse grinned. "Scared, aintchya? If you boys are good, I might let you live a while longer. Some fool might be willing to pay ransom for your sorry tails. Take off them duds and your shoes, so you won't get any ideas about escaping."

"No, we ain't gonna—" Carl protested.

Jesse whacked his mouth with the butt of the heavy revolver, leaving a trickle of blood running down Carl's chin. Carl's eyes went blank, but he did not pass out. We sat down on the floor of the car and pulled off our shoes, then our pants and coats. The fat man kicked me in the ribs. "Shirt, too."

The gang collected more loot from other passengers, then herded us off the train like we were a couple of sheep. I silently thanked Maw for making me wear heavy wool underwear and that she had knitted my stockings out of good

Scottish wool. Fortunately, my stiletto, our only weapon, was still strapped to my ankle under the stocking.

The gang finished stuffing jewelry, greenbacks, and gold pieces into their saddle bags. The big-bellied fellow aimed his pistol at Carl's chest. "C'mon Jessse, lemme kill 'em both right now before we go," he said.

Jesse James looked us over. "Nah. Let's keep 'em as carrots to attract those Pinkerton donkeys. We'll let their stink fill the air. That damn Allan Pinkerton'll come sniffing around. When he does, we'll set a trap and nail that Scottish bastard."

They tied my hands with flat leather thongs and lifted me onto the rump of a horse behind the saddle. When they bound my feet under the horse I was helpless.

They did the same to Carl and we set off on a hard ride. We mucked about through dense woods. Then, one of the gang members yelled to another to go up a stream bed so as not to leave tracks. I tried to forget I was a captive and, instead, imagined I was a character in a great American adventure novel by James Fenimore Cooper. I was not used to praying, but I sure prayed that these desperate men would take pity and turn us loose.

Every so often we stopped so one of the boys could look back for a posse. We were up in the hills where it was colder and snowing. I shivered, and my hands were numb from the tight thongs. It was not until after we came to a ramshackle log cabin that one of the gang finally cut my feet loose. I fell to the hard ground. It hurt, but nothing was broken. We could not walk, so they dragged us into the cabin and shoved us into the corner on the dirt floor. Jesse tied us together with a lariat and hitched one end to a post. We were not going anywhere soon . . .

The musty cabin, lit by one oil lamp, was foul from grease, old sweat, and sour piss. We were tired and thankful to still be alive. I struggled to stay alert and remembered Dr. Bell's admonition to be observant. I hung my head so as not to attract attention, but let my eyes rove around the room, searching for a means of escape. It was a plain log cabin with a low ceiling and two small windows. A table cluttered with whisky bottles and cards was in the middle of the room surrounded by homemade split wood chairs. An iron cookstove and a kitchen counter were near to the door. Straw sleeping pallets were scattered about on the floor, but there was no other furniture. I noticed the gang had hung their coats on pegs by the door, but they kept their guns close by. I did not see any hole where we could slip through and escape. It looked hopeless.

Because we would not be going anywhere soon, Carl and I ultimately gave in to our fatigue, rested our heads upon each other's shoulders, and drowsed off in an exhausted sleep.

25 November, 1878

Come morning, I woke up to the smell of cooking grease and the sound of Carl's snoring. A bedraggled old woman fried corn meal mush, eggs, and pork belly on the stove.

I noticed that the left sleeve of her dark brown dress was pinned up just below the elbow. The poor woman had no forearm.

Carl awoke and blinked the sleep from his eyes. "Look . . ." he said.

In the opposite corner of the cabin, a man tossed and turned on a straw pallet with his foot poking out from under a pile of quilts. The red, swollen foot was partly plastered with a brown mush. The fellow mumbled about escaping from jail and hiding in the woods, but he did not make sense. He was plumb delirious.

I figured they would give us a scrap of food, but Jesse and his gang ignored us. The gang ate their breakfast on the rickety wood table. There was not a morsel left after they were done eating and scraped their plates on the ground outside the door. We heard the sounds of saddles slapped on the backs of their horses, and then hoofbeats, when they rode away.

Carl and I were alone in the cabin with the wounded man and the old lady. As the day progressed, the old lady bustled about while the wounded man moaned and hollered. I had not had anything to drink for almost a whole day, but had to pee so bad, I almost bust. "It's just a dirt floor, let it go," said Carl. I did and felt a lot better. The smell was no worse than the rest of the room.

Just at dusk the gang returned and flung a small deer on the ground. The old lady, with one hand and the stump of her other arm, skinned and gutted the animal while the men smoked and passed a whisky bottle. Later, our mouths watered while the men ate venison stew. We were powerfully hungry, but they did not even give us scraps.

As everybody ate, the room grew warmer and I sensed an opportunity. I pointed at the injured fellow. "What happened to him?" I asked.

"Got shot in the foot after robbin' a bank last week," said Jesse.

"What's that brown stuff his foot is wrapped in?" Carl asked.

"A plaster of chewin' tobacco," said the dark-haired fellow with the big belly, who they called Cole Younger.

"He looks pretty bad. Why don't you let us have a look? I wasn't lying. We really are training to be doctors," I said.

"Just listen to the lies. Ma, do they look like the Pinkertons that killed Archie? I should shoot them right now," said Jesse.

I leaned close to Carl. "What's he talking about?" I asked.

"The Pinkertons thought they had Jesse and his gang trapped and blew up his house, but Jesse got away. They killed his little brother, Archie, and his mother lost her arm. Most folks down here sympathize with him and hate the Pinkertons."

Mrs. James lifted the oil lamp close to our faces with her good hand and looked closely into our eyes. "Naw . . . These are just two scared boys. Don't look like no Pinkertons to me."

Our medical training might save us if we convinced these desperados that we could save the life of the injured man. Trouble was we did not have antiseptics or ether or even clean bandages. But, if given the chance, we could make a show of treating the wound and hope they didn't know the difference.

"We got to string them up anyway, on account of they know too much," Cole Younger said.

The injured man was delirious. He let out a piercing cry of pain.

"Hell, Cole, what's the rush? Maybe they can help Ace. Untie their hands and give them a chance to show what they can do," the old lady said.

Her word was law. Jesse untied our hands and held the lamp while we looked at the foot. The bullet had left a big hole that oozed pus just below the ankle. The whole foot was swollen, red, and hot, with red streaks running up the leg. A chaw of tobacco was sticking out of the hole and tobacco juice was smeared over the wound.

My heart sank right down to my socks. It looked hopeless until Carl spoke up in his best country accent. "Thank you, Ma'am. Now, please boil up a kettle of water and give us a bottle of that there whisky. We'll have your boy right as rain in no time flat!"

We cleaned the wound with soap and water and poured whisky into the jagged hole. It still looked bad. The edges of the skin were green and the sole of the foot bulged out. I thought even Dr. Bell could not help this man.

"There's pus in there," I said.

"Ma'am, we just need us a sharp knife to drain that there pus." Carl said. I thought of the stiletto still strapped to my leg under my long johns, but did not dare mention it.

The old lady hunted through the shelves and came up with a straight razor. "Here, take this. It's sharp, but don't get no ideas. If you even think of using it for anything other than helping Ace, Jesse will blow your head off."

"Yes, ma'am." Carl said.

Carl plunked the razor in the boiling water and then fished it out with a couple of forks. When the razor cooled, Carl felt the swelling and squinted a long time at the evil mess of torn, infected flesh. Ace had passed out from the fever and hardly moved when Carl made a cut that went across the sole of his foot.

I was pretty nervous until he sliced deeper down to bone and about a pint of green stinking pus welled up out of the wound. We poured in more whisky and tied the foot up in a bandanna that had been boiled.

Jesse's mother nodded. "You boys know doctoring alright. Mebbe we should put you to work and keep you around for a while."

"Hell no. Don't make no difference. They seen our faces. We gotta string 'em up in the morning." Jesse said.

"Why wait? Let's have a necktie party right now." Cole Younger, the meanest man of the bunch, waved his pistol.

"No, damn it. Just tie them up," Jesse said. Cole, the drunkest of the gang, tied our hands, but he fumbled the knots. I could have slipped my hands out of the binding, but waited until the gang finished playing cards and drinking whisky. They finally settled down on the dirt floor for the night at what I judged was about one o'clock in the morning.

26 November, 1878

They were snoring up a storm when Carl gave me a nudge. "Doyle, this might be our only chance."

I worked my hands loose and got out the stiletto, then cut the knots on Carl's thongs. He untied my feet and we crawled towards the door. We each took a heavy coat from the pegs and escaped out the door. It had not stopped snowing and it was cold. There was white everywhere, which enabled us to see, but also meant that the gang could easy follow our tracks.

"Let's steal a horse," I said.

"They would catch us in no time. We've got to stay in the deep woods. Listen close. These nights are cold, and the snow half-melts during the day, but freezes over with a crust at night. It will be hard for them to follow us on foot or horseback, but I got an even better idea," Carl whispered. He stopped by an old whisky barrel behind the shed.

"What are you doing?" I whispered.

"Going to make a way for us to slip away on top of the crust and move at a faster clip."

Carl ripped away the rusty metal bands that encircled the barrel and removed four curved staves. We listened to see if the noise had roused the gang, but there was no sign they heard us. Carl sneaked back into the cabin. In a moment, he returned with a skillet covered with old bacon grease and a coat pocket filled with bread and hunks of venison. "There was still food left on the stove," he said. He smeared bacon grease on the bottom of the staves. "Keep those leather thongs. And now take your skis and let's get going," he said.

"Skis? What are skis?"

"Those staves."

"Huh?"

"I'll explain later. Just grab 'em and follow me."

We tramped off through the snow, but it was bloody cold and hard going. We were leaving tracks, but I was more thankful than ever for Maw's heavy wool stockings and the woolly long johns. The stolen coat helped a lot. At the top of a hill, we stopped at a narrow path that led into the woods.

"Use the thongs to tie your feet to the staves and we will zoom down this hill."

"Carl, I have never been on skis," I said.

"Ain't no time for lessons. Do as I do. Aim your feet downhill and push off," he said.

I felt clumsy on the skis and was scared, though I had no choice but to follow Carl down the hill at an alarming speed. We had no more started than I heard shouts and the *BAM! BAM!* of Colt .45 revolvers and the sharp *CRACK!* of a

Winchester rifle. They were probably firing at the noise we made. Even though I am writing this a week later, I can still feel the wind as a bullet whistled next to my ear. Fortunately, the gang was still at least half-drunk, and the muzzle blasts must have ruined their night sight.

We slid into a dense stand of brush and trees and were out of their sight, but the gang still kept shooting.

I fell down in a snow drift and struggled to get back up. "Crouch low, keep the staves parallel, and bend your knees." Carl said. We started down the hill and I fell to the side, but I righted myself and held my arms out to try to not fall.

I started to get the hang of it and imitated Carl, crouched low, and whizzed down the hill. Despite our being earthbound, it felt as if we were flying. I gained speed, but the gang must have heard us again as they started another barrage of gun fire. I heard one bullet whiz through the brush. I ducked, though the bullet was a long ways away.

Carl reached the bottom of the hill first. He stopped himself, discarded his staves, and grabbed me as I zoomed by him. "Get rid of your skis and follow me," Carl said. We took off into the dense woods.

Over the course of my short life, I have spent very little time in the country and no time in the deep woods, so I was not feeling especially confident. After a few minutes we did not hear any more shooting.

The sound of howling replaced the sound of bullets. My thoughts turned to wolves and bears and how they might be more dangerous than the gang. But, Carl was comfortable in the deep woods. He forged ahead through the snow, so I stumbled along in his path.

"Carl, do you know where we are going?"

"Don't worry your Scottish head. This is nothing. Once my little brother and I were hunting and got lost in a snowstorm, but we stayed warm by moving and survived. By the time we got back to the farm my parents thought we were dead. Keep moving. We will find a stream and follow it until it leads to a river. There are always towns on rivers."

It was dark and terrifying in the forest. And cold. My feet felt like they were solid chunks of ice. The only thing that seemed to keep us from freezing was to continue walking and talking. Carl kept up a steady conversation—much ado about nothing—which went something like this:

"Arthur, in a fight, who do you think would win; Natty Bumppo—you know, Hawkeye from *The Last of the Mohicans*—or Ivanhoe from Sir Walter Scott's book?"

"Nobody, Carl. They are both fictional characters."

"I know. But, still, if they were in the woods and had to battle to the death, who do you think would win?"

"I refuse to have this inane conversation, Carl. They are not real people."

"All right, then. If Genghis Kahn and Alexander the Great met each other here in the woods and had to fight to the death, who do you think—"

"They lived in completely different eras. It would be physically impossible for them to ever meet."

"I know. But, still, what if . . ."

He kept me awake and going, but I was exhausted. I, grew careless, and tripped over a root. Carl bent down and offered me a ham-sized hand. "Carl, let's rest here for a few minutes," I pleaded.

I pulled the canvas coat tighter. We huddled close together for warmth and rested a few minutes, but the cold was still brutal. Carl's teeth chattered. "We have to go before we freeze to death," he said.

We struggled on together through the black night. Carl talked and talked so we would stay awake and keep our spirits up. Though we eased our hunger by sharing small bites of the food we had stolen from the James Gang, we had no relief from the cold until the early morning sun warmed our cheeks and the snow started to melt.

We stopped going long enough to sit down with our backs to a chestnut tree and chew some chunks of hard bread and venison. Carl got sort of dreamy and talked about his hopes of marrying a pretty nurse and being a country doctor in Wisconsin. That got me to thinking of Rebecca, and my heart warmed.

We got up, stiff and cold, and kept going until we came to a bubbly creek flowing over smooth sand. Our wool socks were already wet and crusted with ice and snow, so we waded into the creek, figuring it would lead to something bigger. The water felt almost warm; at least it was not freezing. We pushed aside brush and stumbled over stones as we walked. My feet felt almost warm for a spell, but soon were, again, like chunks of ice. By that time, my head was sore and my leg muscles burned. I was in a foul mood and wanted to go back to Scotland. This was a lot more adventure on the American frontier than I had bargained for. Perhaps I did not want to be like an American frontier hero in a James Fenimore Cooper novel after all.

"As long as we continue downstream we will come to a town." Carl was reassuring and I felt better. We rested a while under a big cottonwood tree, soaked up the warm sun, drank cold stream water, and finished off the bread and meat. I would rather have had bacon and eggs.

"Let's get going. If we can figure which way is east, we will come to the Mississippi river after a while, if we don't reach a town first," Carl said.

It was mid-afternoon when the creek went under a bridge on a dirt road. I collapsed with my back against the base of the bridge. "Carl, I'm sorry, but my feet are frozen and I can't go one step further."

He slumped down next to me. After we had been sitting for a wee bit we heard the sound of a wagon creaking down the road. I thought of the James Gang and felt a stab of fear in my gut, but it was only a lad of not more than sixteen years old driving a hay wagon drawn by a sway-backed mule.

"You fellers look plumb worn out," the boy said.

"Worn out, cold, and hungry. We were robbed in a train holdup." Carl said.

"Where you headed?" The lad asked.

"Memphis."

"That's an awfully long walk."

"We were hoping to get to the river. Can you give us a ride?" Carl asked.

"Naw, the load is already too heavy and I got to get this hay to Cape Girardeau."

I looked the boy square in the eye and pulled the stiletto from under my stocking.

He threw up his hands. "Now fellers, don't cut me."

"I don't mean you no harm. I'll trade this knife for a ride and something to eat," I said.

He admired the sharp killing blade, took the knife, and turned it over in his hand. "Well, ok, fellas. Climb on if you want and I'll take ya. And have some bacon. You can lay back there in the hay and cover up with this here blanket."

Cold bacon never tasted better, and the hay and blanket warmed our bones. The cart clacked and bucked its way over the dirt trail while we huddled together to stay warm. I watched the green woods of Missouri pass by until it got dark. The boy pulled off the road and we spent the night, warm as bugs, under the hay.

27 November, 1878

We arrived in Cape Girardeau at around nine o'clock in the morning. The lad, whose name was Travis, gave us bread and molasses for breakfast. It was still cold, so he let us keep the blanket.

We got off the wagon at the livery stable and limped through town towards the river. A pot-bellied fellow with a shiny badge swaggered towards us. He hooked his thumbs in his belt. "We don't want no good-for-nothing tramps in our town. Beat it or go to jail," he said.

"We aren't tramps. My family owns a 400-acre farm in Wisconsin," Carl replied.

"You damn well look like tramps. Get the hell out of town."

We skedaddled on out of town to the steamboat landing on the great muddy Mississippi River.

I sat on a bench overlooking the river, and, after a few minutes, fell asleep. Carl went off talking to the roustabouts until he met a bloke from Wisconsin who got us a job shoveling coal on a decrepit little cargo steamboat. The Captain was glad to have new hands and gave us some old clothes to wear. We were still in our stocking feet, but did not look any worse than the other coal stokers.

We took turns all day shoveling coal into the furnace to keep the steam boiler going. The boat chugged along, stopping every so often to take on bags of grain bound for Memphis. Whenever we could, we snuck out to the deck to get a glimpse of our surroundings and watch the river roll by.

I wanted to write about the journey, but did not have paper or pencil. Instead, I froze the river, the flocks of ducks, and the muddy banks in my memory for a future story. Whenever the fire got low, the first mate cussed and threatened to throw us overboard. I threw big chunks of wood and coal on the fire and ran back on deck so as not to miss anything.

When our shift was over the first mate let us eat leftovers, mostly fried catfish and cornbread. We drank river water after the mud settled and bedded down on grain sacks where we slept like dead men.

28 November, 1878

We did shifts in the morning and afternoon until, in the distance, I made out buildings and tall church steeples up on a bluff. Memphis looked like a fine city, but down by the river there were tumbled-down stores and shacks on muddy streets.

The deckhands lowered the gangplank down onto a cobblestone landing where steamboats were lined up for near a half-mile. The mate gave us burlap bags to wrap around our feet. "I'll pay you two bits apiece if you help us unload," he said.

Carl and I readily agreed. We fell in with the black deckhands and passed the hundred-pound sacks of corn to the next man in the line up to the warehouse. I was strong from playing rugger and rounders, but it was bloody hard work.

Big Bart, a six-foot-four black man, was the leader of the workers. "You the first white boys I seen who know how to work," he said.

We all jollied and joked and had a pretty good time. After we collected our two dimes and a nickel I sat next to Bart who offered me an apple.

"You sound British?" he asked, as we ate together.

"I'm of Irish blood, but I'm studying medicine in Scotland."

"So what brings you to these parts?"

"We were robbed by the James Gang. Lost everything and we need help. A friend said we should see Mr. Josiah Burk in Memphis. Ever hear of him?"

"No." Bart turned cold and distant. "I don't know no Mr. Burk."

"Well, do you at least know where Second Street is?"

"Don't know that neither."

Bart got up to leave, but I grabbed his shoulder. I showed him the black spot on my wrist. He paused and squinted. "Who made that mark on you?"

"My friend, Rufus Bubba Freeman."

"He must have been a slave at one time."

"Yes. That's right. He used to be known as Rufus Bedford Forrest."

His face crinkled with a big smile. "Hmmm… In that case, you keep on this here road until you are up on the bluff and come to Second Street. Turn right and go down a ways. Mr. Burk lives in the white house."

It was near dark when we found the white cottage surrounded by old trees.

"We better go around to the back door, especially considering we're still wearing these dirty old rags from the steamer," Carl said.

I hung back and let Carl do the talking when a little old lady opened the door just a little. "You men looking for food?" she asked.

"No, Ma'am, I'm a Wisconsin farm boy and now, we're medical students coming to help with the epidemic. We were robbed and come to see Mr. Josiah Burk," Carl said.

The lady opened the door another few inches and squinted at us through little half-rim spectacles. She could not have stood more than five feet tall. She wore a bonnet and a long calico dress buttoned up to her neck.

"Land-sakes, you boys look a fright."

I guess we did look pretty bad. My shirt and trousers were soot-covered and torn. The fact that we did not have shoes made us look worse than the usual tramp. Carl was in just as bad a shape and neither one of us had washed or combed our hair in a week. "Come in, come in and I'll call my husband," she said in a kindly soft voice.

She took us into her warm, cheery kitchen lit by two oil lamps and heated with a big iron cookstove. We both drooled at the sight of a big piece of ham, a loaf of bread, and a bowl of apples on the table.

"Josiah, two boys are here to see you."

Mr. Burk was a stout man with hair gone to grey and dressed in a black frock coat, shiny black trousers, and a white shirt. He looked solemn enough to be a minister, but, after he said thee and thou a few times, we learned that he and his wife were Quakers. I held out my wrist towards the lamp so that they could see the tiny black spot.

"Remarkable. I have never seen that mark on a white man."

"A black man said we could trust you," I said.

He stroked his beard. "Mrs. Burk and I helped many a slave to freedom before the war."

The Burks took us in and gave us supper. Mrs. Burk drew a hot bath. After Carl scrubbed down with rough, homemade soap I jumped in while the water was still hot. It felt so good to be clean and warm. Our bedroom was a lean-to out back with only one sofa. Carl took the floor. "Sleeping on a nice warm hardwood floor is nothing," he said. "Back on the farm, we had so little room in the house, I'd often sleep on the dirt floor of our chicken coop."

In minutes, Carl snored. I could not sleep, so I wandered to the kitchen. Mrs. Burk was reading a religious tract. I slumped down on a wooden kitchen chair across from her.

She had white hair and watery, sad grey eyes that reminded me of my dear, poor mother.

Mrs. Burk poured boiling water from a copper kettle onto dry tea leaves in a plain white cup. "Drink this," she said.

It was a dark, strangely soothing brew. In a moment, I emptied the cup and felt drowsy. She took the cup, swirled the remaining leaves, and looked intently at the bottom and sides of the cup.

Her old grey eyes took on a new luminosity. I sensed a change in the room and the intensity of her gaze. "You are troubled by a dark, inky past. For a young man, you've experienced great sadness and much death. It's your Irish blood and the Romani blot." Her voice was a mere whisper, but every word went into my very soul.

I shivered at the memories of the harsh beatings and my rigid education at the hands of the Jesuits when I was a boy. I had forsaken religion for science, a move that caused my Maw great sorrow.

Mrs. Burk looked back down into my teacup. "I see an older woman—dying. Your grandmother, perhaps. You're just a young boy, crying at her bedside."

The shock of my grandmother's death came back with the full force I had felt while still a young boy. Her passing started our family on the path to poverty and ruin, and it was the reason I was sent away to live with relatives and the Jesuits.

"Now I see another woman, a wisp of a girl, but beautiful. She tugs at your heart, but she is not of your faith and would bring great sadness to your mother. You must not marry her."

I came alert with a start. My mind whirled. Did this old woman have the gift of second sight? Could she see the past and divine the future? My scientific background and Jesuit teaching told me no. But, then, was she speaking of my dear Rebecca? I was overcome with shame and guilt that took my breath away. I had abandoned the faith of my parents, and I had eagerly run away on this trip, leaving them in their poverty. I should have stayed in Edinburgh to help out.

I felt awful. How could I be such a bad son? I stumbled away and sank into bed.

29 November, 1878

I awoke on the sofa to the smell of bacon and sausages that reminded me of home. It took a minute to realize I was in the middle of perilous America. Mrs. Burk had generously mended our clothes, so we looked halfway decent for the first time in days. The Burks also had a storeroom with old clothes and shoes for runaway slaves that they now shared with poor travelers like us. I found a pair of boots that almost fit. A little lamp black made them look respectable.

"So, you boys want to use your medical learning to help with the yellow fever?" Mr. Burk inquired while we were at breakfast.

"Yes, sir," we answered.

"The epidemic is almost over, but there still are sick folks at St. Mary's who need help."

"Was there a lot of fighting around here during the war?" I asked.

"Oh yes. The Union took Memphis early in the war, then the Rebels raided the fort several times," Mr. Burk said.

"Ever hear of a Confederate officer named Captain Hook?"

"He was bad. A very bad man. Funny you mention him. I just overheard some folks saying that he is rallying his old troops to make mischief again."

I felt the urge to record this information and my experiences, but had neither pencil nor paper. "Sir, I can do chores or give you a nickel for a notebook or a pad of paper and a pencil."

Mr. Burk rummaged through an old rolltop desk and produced a pad of cheap foolscap and a pencil stub. "It's worth a nickel," he said.

I thanked him, took the paper, and offered to do chores, but he sent us on our way with handshakes and smiles.

We could see the church from a long ways away. The imposing St. Mary's was a big stone structure with a high steeple that had been made into a hospital. The yellow fever epidemic might have been nearly over, but there were still at least fifty poor, sick souls lying on cots in front of the altar. A nun in starchy white met us at the door. She looked us over with a critical eye.

"Do you boys have medical experience?" she asked.

"Yes, Ma'am. We are medical students and want to help."

She pointed to a heap of wrapped bodies. "First thing, carry out the ones that died last night."

The corpses were already wrapped in sheets, so we could not tell what they looked like, but they were light as a feather. When we finished stacking the bodies on the cart like so much cordwood, another sister gave us buckets of water and towels to clean new patients.

All day, we cleaned black vomit, changed beds, and held patient's heads while they took broth. It was more like nursing than medical work, but it felt good to help these unfortunate souls. No matter how awful my problems seemed to be, these folks had it much worse.

The new patients were out of their heads with fever, their teeth chattered from chills, and they bled from their mouths, eyes, and noses. The skin of the some patients had turned yellow, and even I could see that many were doomed to die from kidney or liver failure.

It was late afternoon when Carl and I took a break and rested on a cot. A nice-looking lady holding a pot of coffee walked over to us and sat down next to us. "You boys must be plum tuckered out. Have some coffee," she said.

"Thank you, ma'am," said Carl.

She poured each of us a cup. "This is the first time I have seen you boys."

"We're medical students from Chicago," I said.

"They say the epidemic is about over. Good thing, since my gals are getting tired of seeing these poor folks die every day. The sisters pray for their souls, but there ain't much else we can do," she said.

"It's awfully hard, but important, work," I added.

"Where are you boys staying?"

"We don't have lodgings yet," I said.

"If you behave and leave my girls alone, I can give you a meal and make room for you at my place. Go to Angie's Hotel on First Street right on your way to the docks. Go in by the back door and say Angie sent you."

"That's very kind," I said.

"There was a nurse with a funny accent like yours who was here yesterday."

"Did she happen to have flaming red curly hair and sparkling green eyes?" I asked.

"Why, yes, she did."

"Was her name Rebecca?"

"I think so."

My heart skipped a beat. "Do you happen to know where she might be staying?"

"She didn't say."

I had vowed to give up on Rebecca, especially after Mrs. Burk's strange message that had gone straight to my heart. Yet I could not get her out of my mind as I blindly followed Carl through darkened streets. It was raining and the wind was whistling off the river when we finally came to First Street.

The area was mostly lit by red lanterns in front of dismal shacks and saloons. Angie's Hotel was a higher-class place, though not by much. The kitchen was clean, but the cook, an old black lady with an enormous apron across her fat belly, was not very friendly.

"Why ain't you usin' the front door, like every other man?" she asked

"Angie sent us here."

"I 'spose you wants eats?"

"Aye, a bit of food would be much appreciated," said I.

"I kin give you beef stew and fixin's for fifteen cents."

We shelled out thirty cents in dimes and nickels and tucked into beef stew, homemade biscuits, and gravy served out of tin plates at the kitchen table. The cook sat with us. "These are the best vittles I've had in a long time," Carl said.

She smiled for the first time. "You kin call me Ma, like all the girls. You boys is more polite than most men who come here. Would you like a helpin' of apple pie?" she asked.

"Yes ma'am," I said.

She served up two slabs of pie filled with sliced apples, cinnamon, and sugar. "Oh, I've never, even at home, had such good pie," said Carl.

"Yes, it is quite lovely," I added.

"Nobody ever called my pie lovely 'afore," she said.

"How's business?" Carl asked.

She sighed. "Ain't been much of anything you can call business since the epidemic, 'cept last night when a crowd of old Confederates come nosin' around. I din't like them fellers at all."

We were scraping the bottoms of our plates and licking our spoons when a little, blonde, skinny girl flounced into the kitchen wearing a wide-open, tiny housecoat without a stitch of underclothes except for black stockings and loose slippers. She was no more than sixteen years old if she was a day. The girl acted like we were not even there. "Ma, kin you let me have a pitcher of warm water for washin'?" she asked.

The cook filled her pitcher from a bucket on the stove. Then, the little, blonde girl acted like she had just noticed us. "Oh my. Well, hello there, gentlemen. Are you boys lookin' for fun?"

Carl and I smiled shyly. "Sorry, ma'am, but you see we're Pinkerton agents on official railway business," said I.

"I don't care if you're the crown prince of Wales. You oughta be in the front room with the girls."

Carl cleared his throat, but could not speak. She gave Carl a lascivious smile, twitched her hips, and sat down on his lap. "Hello there curly. You big, beautiful, sweet boy. Do you mind if I sit down for a minute?" She kicked a leg back and forth and played with a lock of Carl's hair.

"Um, eh . . . Ah . . ." Carl stammered.

"Curly, I ain't got nothin' to do to-night and I'm sure lonely. Why don't you follow me to my room? I can sure show you a good time . . ."

Carl's face turned beet-red and his jaw started to work, but all that came out of his mouth was hemming and hawing. "Hmm . . . Emm . . . Ummm . . . Ah, sorry, ma'am. You seem nice and all, but we best be on our way." Carl jerked up to his feet and the little girl practically fell to the floor.

"Now, Curly, you ain't very sociable."

"You can stay as long as you want and socialize, but I got things to do." Carl said to me.

Carl burst out the front door. I was sort of reluctant to leave, but followed him into a pouring rain. Carl's face was still flushed with a rosy hue and I could not help but laugh at him.

"What's so funny?"

"I've seen you stand up to Jesse James, but one little girl made you squirm like a wee lad with ants in his knickers," I teased.

"Well, um, eh, that there place is one of those houses of ill repute. We might have gotten a disease if we stayed there too much longer," said Carl.

"Carl, you can't catch venereal diseases from food and furniture."

"Still, it was, um . . . Well . . . I've never done . . . You know . . . and I'm gonna save myself for my wedding night, and I don't wanna talk about this no more!"

Misty halos formed around the gaslights and the eery light made for a dreadfully unnerving feeling. I looked back over my shoulder at every little noise and jumped at the clatter of hooves and jingling spurs. A troop of fifteen or twenty men on horseback cantered down the street, two abreast. Every man wore a long red shirt, carried a rifle, and had a set, dark expression.

"Keep your head down and walk straight ahead," Carl said.

"Who are those men?"

"Red Shirts. One of the White Militias that go night-riding to scare the blacks."

I grabbed Carl and pulled him into an alley. "Carl, people are talking about Confederates. I thought the war was over years ago."

"The war over slavery didn't really end. The Southerners won't give the black people equal rights. They don't let them vote and, in the end, they want to restore slavery. They say the Republicans stole the last election and Northerners are sick of the whole thing and don't really care what happens."

"So, in a way, the war is still going on."

"You might say that . . . Now, we have to secure our lodgings and get out of this rain."

"Dr. Bell said we should go to the Peabody Hotel."

"We've only got ten cents apiece."

"Never mind. It won't hurt to try."

The Peabody was about the swankiest place in Memphis, but we walked right up to the desk like we always stayed in the finest hotels all our lives. "Hello, dear sir. Might there be any messages for Mr. Arthur Conan Doyle?" I asked.

"Why yes, sir." The clerk, without batting an eye, took an envelope and a key with a tag numbered 215 from a cubby hole. The envelope was stuffed with greenbacks, enough for a week's pay for both of us, and a scrap of paper with two words: 'Keep quiet.'

The door to room 215 was unlocked and did not make a sound when I pushed it open. To our great astonishment, a tall, thin man smoking a Meerschaum pipe, sat with a binaural stethoscope pressed against the wall. It was Dr. Bell. And there was good old Rufus, squatting on his haunches, shining shoes. He had stayed with Dr. Bell just as he promised.

Bell put his finger to his lips, motioning for us to be quiet, and offered the stethoscope to me. I adjusted the ear pieces and pressed the bell against the wall to hear snatches of conversation and the tinkling of glasses. *"Why not just shoot him . . . It must appear to be a natural death . . . It is perfected . . . That bastard in Chicago knows . . . The depot in . . ."*

I could not make out all the words, but Dr. Bell had a page full of notes. Carl gasped when he saw the names: Wade Hampton, Jubal Early, Martin Cary. We moved away from the wall and spoke in whispers.

"Those are names of Lee's Confederate generals who never surrendered," Carl said.

"They are plotting assassinations as we speak," Dr. Bell said.

There were more notes, something about a Reverend, that I could not make out. "It sounds as if they are planning more assassinations with the curare poison," I said.

Then an awful thought crossed my mind. If 'that bastard in Chicago' was Dr. Bell, his life was in great danger.

Or maybe, they were referring to me . . .

I am in my own space now and the others are asleep. Dr. Bell thoughtfully brought my precious diary, so I am setting down everything I remember since leaving Chicago. This is a strange land, so different from Scotland. American doctors still do not believe in the germ theory and reject Lister's antiseptic surgery. After thinking about our narrow escape the James Gang is not so different from the highland robbers so prominent in our Scottish lore.

Aye, we are in danger, but even forbidden thoughts of Rebecca, and the possibility of seeing her again, are a tonic.

2 December, 1878

Early this morning, Carl and I went to the cathedral and I asked about the red-haired Scottish beauty. "Try President's Island. There are more patients quarantined there," a nursing sister finally told me.

Carl and I spent some of our salary on new clothes, cigars, and beer and sandwiches in a saloon, where we listened to the gossip. Recalling our original plan, we let it be known that we were Pinkertons working for the railroad. Everyone shied away as soon as they heard our accents, and one fellow called us *damn carpetbaggers*. After we left the saloon Carl went back to the cathedral, but I hurried down to the landing to catch a ferry to President's Island.

Once on the island I walked into what seemed to be an old warehouse, which is now a makeshift hospital filled with the worst cases. I looked down a long corridor filled with beds and she was there! Her red hair stood out like a bright star in a dark evening sky.

"Miss Yates?"

She looked up from wiping vomit off a small lad and tossed a limp lock of hair from her eyes. Her voice was dull and tired. "Oh, Arthur, is it really you?"

"Yes, it is me. I found you."

"Oh, Arthur." She fell into my arms and sobbed. "They're all dead. Jimmy is the only one alive."

I held her and tried to soothe her anxiety. It took several moments for me to understand. The Reverend and Mrs. Balfour had died of yellow fever. Jimmy, their son, was here and near death. The poor boy was feverish, delirious. I could barely feel his pulse.

"Rebecca, please, come with me. You are so tired and in danger of contracting this terrible disease."

"No, I must stay with Jimmy to the end."

I begged her to come with me. Dr. Bell would surely look after her and Jimmy, but she insisted on staying with the sick child.

I was torn between staying with Rebecca and going back to Carl and Dr. Bell. I, too, had a duty.

"Do you have a place to stay?" I asked.

"Yes, with the Reverend Beecher who is also not well. I am needed here."

"I shall bring Dr. Bell to see Jimmy," I said.

I hugged her and left to catch the ferry back to Memphis. Was it fate? Had this terrible disease led to our reunion?

It was dusk when the boat touched the dock in Memphis. As we moored a steam launch backed out into the river. In the fading light, I could make out a tattered sign on the launch which read—SHERLOCK-MEMPHIS LINE.

The word 'Sherlock' startled me.

I paused for a moment and thought of the bloody words, *cinnte faoi ghlas.* Sure lock. And now, here it was again, that strange word. Sherlock.

I jumped onto the dock. As the launch steamed downriver, nosing against waves with its stack belching smoke, I sprinted down the dock to see the sign better and ensure that my mind was not playing tricks on me.

The launch was already too far away to read the sign again. I turned to a grey-bearded black man who was fishing with a long cane pole at the edge of the dock. "Excuse me, sir, may I ask—did you see that boat, the one that said Sherlock?"

The old man merely looked down at the worn wooden planks of the dock. "I don't want no trouble, sir," said he.

Then, he pulled in his line, picked up a can of worms, and hurried away.

I chased after him. "Please, sir, is that boat going to Sherlock?"

"Leave me 'lone. I don't know nothing about no Sherlock." He said these words and disappeared down an alley.

I returned to the docks, questioned two stevedores, and received a similar response. Everyone seemed frightened of the very name, Sherlock. It was most peculiar and mysterious.

Could it be the same name that Fogarty had written with his bloody, dying hand? I would have asked more questions. Instead, I dashed to the cathedral to find Carl. He was still there, spooning broth into the mouth of an old man. After he had finished we hurried back to the hotel as I told him about Sherlock.

When we arrived back at the Peabody Hotel, it was quite late and Dr. Bell and Rufus had already retired.

3 December, 1878

At six o'clock this morning, Bell was up reading his newspapers and drinking coffee. We knocked on his door to let him know about what had transpired. Rufus was putting a final polish on his boots.

"Sir, I found Rebecca Yates. The Balfours are dead from the fever and Jimmy is very ill. Rebecca is looking after the boy on President's Island."

Before I could tell him about Sherlock, he held up his hand. "Oh, so sad, so sad. The Balfour clan is one of the most important in Scotland. We must save Jimmy's life."

"But, sir, your identity will become known if—"

"Never mind, Doyle, my lad. A life is at stake. Bring my instrument case. Doyle, Carl, we will need both of you. We leave at once."

Dr. Bell hailed a cab. "Hurry, man, to the ferry landing." The ferry was not running. Dr. Bell dropped his disguise and became the commanding presence I knew so well.

"Hello!" he shouted at men on a fishing boat. "A ten dollar gold piece for a ride to President's Island."

"Who is in charge?" Bell shouted as we entered the makeshift hospital.

There was no answer. Dr. Bell went from one poor wretch lying in putrid vomit to another. Before our very eyes, an old woman threshed about with fever, chills, and delirium.

"Damn, this is intolerable. We would never stand for this neglect of the sick in Edinburgh."

Then, like a beacon of light, we came to Rebecca, still at Jimmy's bedside. Her lovely face was streaked with tears and she was worn from overwork. Carl, my big unfettered friend, appeared to be struck dumb when he saw her.

Without a word, Dr. Bell threw off his coat and knelt by Jimmy. The lad was delirious with fever and crying weakly for his mother. His lips were parched and cracked, and his eyes were sunk into his head. It was a dreadful sight. One did not have to be a trained surgeon to see that the lad was near to death.

"When did he last drink?" Dr. Bell asked.

"He hasn't had a drop of liquid since yesterday morning. I have tried, but he will not swallow," Rebecca responded.

"We must get him out of here. This is no place for a Scots lad of the great Balfour clan to die. Doyle, wrap the lad in my coat."

I bundled Jimmy and carried him in my arms. Dr. Bell led our little party out of the quarantine hospital and down a muddy path to our boat.

Dr. Bell steadied the boat while I gently put Jimmy on a seat next to Rebecca. "Doyle, where can we find a quiet place with clean linens, drink, and food?" he asked.

I thought for a second. "There is the cathedral, but it's just as crowded as the quarantine hospital. Everyone in the city is frightened of the disease."

"There must be someplace we can go."

"Let me think . . . Well, aye . . . Carl and I met a woman, Angie, a kindly soul, runs a sort of a hotel which is not far away."

"It would not be proper," Carl said.

"Never mind, Angie's is the only place," said I.

As we burst into the front room of Angie's Hotel the half-clothed girls screamed, but, when they saw the sick lad, the girls shed tears and helped us up to Angie's room on the second floor. All the while, Dr. Bell gave no evidence that he was shocked by the licentiousness around him.

Angie's room was opulent, with a brightly lit gold chandelier, a frilly four-poster bed, paintings of cherubs on the wall, and a large plaster saint in a lighted niche. Dr. Bell rolled up his sleeves and went to work. "Doyle, soak sheets in cold water and bring a pitcher of lemonade with sugar and salt."

The young girls of the house scurried about fetching sheets and pitchers of ice water. Rebecca soaked the linens in icy water. Carl and I wrapped Jimmy in the sheets. "Hurry! Where is the lemonade? And bring chicken bouillon," said Dr. Bell.

A particularly fetching lass, wearing only a shift, ran into the kitchen and helped Ma, the old black cook, make enough lemonade for half the city. Then Ma took up a kitchen cleaver, went into the backyard, and killed a chicken to make the broth.

We forced lemonade, fortified with malt whisky, between Jimmy's lips. Most of the drink spilled down his chin, but, eventually, he took the liquid. His teeth chattered with the cold, and his skin took on a bluish tinge, though his temperature receded.

"Ah, we must not go too far. Now, we shall apply warmth," said Dr. Bell.

The girls filled brass bed warmers with hot ashes from the fireplace. We removed the icy sheets, and, with the warmers and blankets, we warmed the boy until Dr. Bell was satisfied.

We continued the vigil through the day and into the night. Rebecca slept, slumped in a chair, while we took turns at the bedside spooning lemonade and broth into the boy.

4 December, 1878

Carl was on duty during the dark, wee hours of the morning when human vitality is at its lowest. Jimmy gave one last small sigh and stopped breathing.

Carl put his hand on the boy's chest. "No! The poor fella . . . He stopped breathing!" he shouted.

Dr. Bell, who was sleeping in a rocking chair, came awake, leaped to Jimmy's side, placed his mouth over the lad's, and forced his own breath into the child's lungs.

After a few moments—moments that seemed like an eternity—Jimmy took a breath, then another. We continued the vigil, which seemed more and more like a death watch. But, in the morning, when sun came streaming through the window, he was no worse.

I had my hand on his feeble pulse. Carl and Dr. Bell closed their eyes and had forty winks. Ma tip-toed into the room with a pitcher of strong root tea. "This is an Indian remedy. Us slaves used it for the fever."

Rebecca and I took turns forcing spoonfuls of the murky brown liquid down Jimmy's throat. By mid-morning, his eyes fluttered and his pulse was stronger. He swallowed more tea and lemonade then drifted into a quiet sleep. By mid-afternoon, Jimmy was able to take an entire cupful of broth and his cheeks gained a hint of a pink glow.

They said it was a miracle that a child so young had survived a bout of yellow fever. The young ladies of the house were in and out of the sick room, sometimes bringing little treats. But, mostly, they fluttered about Carl, playing with his curly hair and making him blush.

Dr. Bell quietly shared a dram of malt whisky with Angie, but I had eyes only for Rebecca. I thought it was the Indian tea, but Dr. Bell scoffed and said it was the salt and whisky in the lemonade that cured little Jimmy. However, I noticed that he put a sample vial of the murky brown liquid in his medical bag. I would wager that he was going to bring it back to Edinburgh for analysis.

When we left, Angie and her girls made a fuss over the lad. The little blonde girl curled his hair and planted a big kiss on Carl who seemed to have lost his fear of 'painted ladies'.

Mr. Payne, the Reverend Beecher's host, sent a regal carriage for Rebecca and Jimmy. I wrapped Jimmy in blankets and carried him into the carriage. Rebecca insisted that I accompany them to the Payne's grand mansion.

Half an hour later, we drove through the stately gates and into a grove of old Rowan Oak trees. It seemed as if we rode for another mile until we finally reached the three-story brick mansion. The proud façade featured porticos, tall windows, and a wide veranda. A servant opened the door and welcomed Rebecca.

I carried Jimmy to a third floor room once occupied by the Balfour family. The lad cried for his parents and was weak as a newborn kitten, but his body was mending well.

"The Reverend Beecher will be stopping by in a moment. I'd like you to meet him," said Rebecca.

I had heard and read a good deal about this Reverend Beecher. His sister was the author of *Uncle Tom's Cabin,* and his adultery trial in 1874 was the most famous of the century. In his prime, the Reverend was a tall, handsome fellow with a high forehead and flowing black locks that hung down below his ears.

It was told that, during his long sermons, Beecher howled high-flown moral platitudes, used slang and humor, banged his fists, and stamped his feet. Even though he was more than fifty years old, he was rumored to still have dashing looks and the romantic air about him of a much younger man. Like many of the women who heard his sermons, I wondered if Rebecca had amorous thoughts about the old lecher.

When the Reverend Henry Ward Beecher greeted us, I was struck by his pallor and how different he looked from what I had imagined. His skin was dry and he lacked vitality. He was sickly, moved with difficulty, and his breathing was labored. He held out a quavering hand when Rebecca introduced me as Dr. Bell's assistant.

"Ah, Mr. Doyle, I am pleased to meet you. Mrs. Balfour regaled us with her praises of you and Dr. Bell. I wonder—is it a coincidence, or God's divine will, that you and the great doctor are here in this very city? My fondest wish is to have a medical consultation with him."

"Sir, I am sorry, but—"

"I am not as young as I used to be and I must gather my strength. I have to complete my great work."

"Dr. Bell is not seeing patients right now."

"Yet, he just saved the life of young Master Balfour."

"He would prefer if you kept that to yourself. Please don't mention his presence in this city."

"Even better. We shall have a clandestine consultation and it will be our little secret. You see, I need his opinion on my treatment. My physician has great faith in glandular extracts, but I want Bell's opinion."

"Who, may I ask, is your physician?"

"Dr. Edward Droussard."

I was taken aback. "Sir, do you mean Emilie Droussard?"

"Not Emilie. Edward. He has a most brilliant scientific mind and he is most up to date in his practice."

"Still, I believe that Dr. Bell can't—"

Beecher grabbed my shoulder. "Droussard is providing me with the very latest treatments to restore my vigor and endow me with eternal youth, but I want to seek counsel from Dr. Bell."

"But—"

He shook me. "I TRUST YOU WILL ARRANGE THIS, YES?"

For an apparently ill man, his grip was quite strong. "Um, aye sir. I will relay your desire for a consultation to Dr. Bell. If he does agree, I hope you understand that he must remain incognito," said I.

"Excellent . . . Ah, to fly about as if I was a young boy again," the Reverend Beecher said, with a smile.

I offered my farewell to Miss Yates, but she was preoccupied with Jimmy and did not even wish me well.

I was devastated by the cruel, cold distance that she had imposed between us, but I pretended to not be hurt, held my head high, and made my way back to the carriage, never once looking back.

5 December, 1878

After breakfast Carl and I spent the day wandering around Memphis, trying to discover more about Sherlock. We came up empty-handed. It was not until dinner at the Peabody Hotel with Dr. Bell and Rufus that we learned more of the sinister plot of our foes.

"Doyle, did you observe anything of import in town today?" Dr. Bell asked.

"No, sir. Unfortunately, it was a day of constant cul-de-sacs or, as Carl would say, 'dead ends.' "

"Well, one would have been better off spending one's time investigating those places where the walls have ears."

"I don't follow, sir."

"My dear Doyle, sometimes the apparently most common personage might provide the one missing clue necessary to unravel a mystery. For instance, all day long, Angie, that most estimable of hotel keepers, happens to be privy to some most damning conversations."

"My Lord." Carl could not control himself and jumped up. "What'd she say?"

"Well, Carl, if you'd just calm yourself, I shall tell you. You see, on more than one occasion, she has overheard former Confederate officers talk of overthrowing the government of the United States. They only lack a charismatic leader to convince the Northern states to repeal the Thirteenth Amendment that freed the slaves. They hope that this leader, whoever he is, will become the next President of the United States."

"But, sir, that is not possible. There are too many good, God-fearing people in this country to allow such a thing to occur."

"Sorry Arthur, but that's not true." Carl shook his head. "Most Northerners are still sick of war and not interested in the plight of former slaves. Many of our leaders are conciliatory towards the Southern whites."

"But, how could—"

Dr. Bell cleared his throat. "Doyle, consider the politics of our day. The most prominent minister in the land, The Reverend Henry Ward Beecher, is preaching Darwin's theory of survival of the fittest. He has renounced his former abolitionist views and thinks the blacks would be better off as slaves under benevolent owners at least until the twentieth century."

"Speaking of the Reverend Beecher, I met him when I went I returned Miss Yates and Jimmy to their lodgings."

"Doyle, you must tell me these things."

"I did not tell you because I know how you want to remain incognito here in Memphis and, well, he was begging for a consultation with you about his glandular treatments."

"Ah yes . . . It is all starting to make sense." The good doctor took a puff from his Meerschaum pipe and exhaled a cloud of smoke. "I appreciate you trying to protect me, Doyle, but, indeed, I shall be more than happy to advise the Reverend. In fact, it might be the only way we may learn more about this curious case."

"Maybe you can do better than us. We spent the whole day trying to learn more about a ferry boat with a sign, 'SHERLOCK-MEMPHIS'."

"Hmmm… Tell me what you observed."

"Well, when we saw it, I thought that maybe this might be the same 'sure lock' that Fogarty wrote about in his blood."

Dr. Bell sprung from his chair. "Bravo, Doyle. You have found another piece of the puzzle. Aye, of course. The poor man, in his death throes, wrote the word Sherlock in Gaelic. It must be the name of a town or village. Rufus, get busy. Ask your new friends here in town about this name."

"Yes, sir, I'll ask my lady friend. She'll know."

"But, Mr. Freeman, isn't she in Chicago?"

"Oh, I gots a lady friend here, too."

Everybody at the table laughed. I winked at him. "Mr. Freeman, you sly devil, you," I said.

Rufus looked coy and laughed with embarrassment. . .

6 December, 1878

In the morning, Carl and I arranged for Dr. Bell to see the Reverend Beecher. Rufus spent a few hours in town trying to get more information about the place known as Sherlock.

During lunch, Rufus gave his report. "I had to pay a dollar 'afore anyone talked. Some folks say the place is cursed. Others say it be a house with haunts. Even white folks won't go there."

"Bosh, that just sounds like a bunch of old wives tales," I said.

"No, suh. It's the truth. Sherlock was once a rich cotton plantation on a piece of low land dat jutted into the river, but da river come up and wash most of it away. A few years later, during high water, da river cut a channel dat made the tip of the land into an island, and then, well . . ."

Suddenly, he shifted his feet, his body tensed, and he shook nervously. "I can'ts tell you no more. No, suh . . ." Dear Rufus, who was our intellectual equal and had learned anatomy and physiology, had become scared, superstitious, and was talking like he was still a slave.

"Please Mr. Freeman, there is no need to get alarmed. If you will be so kind, tell us more . . . What is on the island now?" Dr. Bell asked.

"Dat island is done gone and growed up with weeds and bramble thickets and dey's rattlesnakes and wild beasts that walk on two feet and screech somethin' fierce. Everybody says ain't no people left there, but dey's an old, scarlet-colored plantation house on a hill with a buncha other little old cabins next to it. Da black folks say ghosts of dead Confederate soldiers live dere and when dey's a full moon, da walls of dat place run red with blood, and lights flicker, and Lucifer's smoke pours outta all the winders of dat ole place."

"Hmmm . . . I would like to visit this island. Where exactly did you say it is?" Dr. Bell asked.

"'Bout fifteen miles downriver."

"We must reconnoiter there this afternoon."

"No suh." Rufus twisted his cap and rolled his eyes. "No, suh, Docta Bell, dat ain't a good idea."

"I understand. I appreciate your concern, but it is imperative that I pay this island a visit. Please tell me how to find it. Can we take that ferry boat?"

"It don't go there no more."

"But, Doyle said that it had a sign which read—"

"Dat sign on da steam boat musta been from de old days."

With a flurry of orders, Dr. Bell arranged for a suitable vessel to take us all to inspect Sherlock. Rufus agreed to come only if he did not have to get out of the boat. Dr. Bell said that we must stop at Payne's mansion on the way to the dock so that he might have a consultation with the Reverend Beecher.

Rufus hailed a cab and we all set off to the mansion. "Are you really certain that visiting the Reverend Beecher is a good idea, sir?" I asked Dr. Bell.

He patted my arm and smiled. "Why, Miss Yates should be there, Doyle. Don't you want to see her?"

"I, um . . . Well, aye, but, still . . ."

"Doyle, a truly dangerous plot is afoot." Dr. Bell paused, lit his pipe, and exhaled a fragrant cloud of smoke. "We must see Beecher. He may be the only one who can lead us to the heart of this mystery and to the sinister mind that lurks behind all of these deaths."

"That makes sense, sir, but, how, then, is all this connected to Sherlock, an uninhabited island?"

"If what I have deduced is correct, Doyle, you will soon see for yourself."

Half an hour later, we arrived at the Payne mansion. Rufus refused to go inside. "Dem folks owned 'bout a thousand slaves 'afore the war and dey still treats black folks bad," he said. Carl decided to stay with him, so it was just Dr. Bell and I who knocked on the door. A few moments later, the Reverend Beecher ushered us inside.

He appeared weak, but he talked eagerly of his upcoming operation as he walked Dr. Bell to the library. "Doctor Bell, have you ever read Ovid's Metamorphoses?"

"Aye, of course. Why do you ask?"

"Well, do you remember Ovid's retelling of the myth of the child-god Iacchus?"

"Aye, the puer aeternus—the eternal boy who never grows old."

"This myth has always meant a great deal to me because as a young boy in Litchfield, Connecticut, I had a dear, dear friend, Peter, who died at the tender age of eight. He was such a sweet, gentle soul. He was musical and loved to play the pan pipes. When a child dies so young, in the minds of those who loved him he never grows old. It is as if sweet Peter lives on in a never, never land where he is a puer aeternus—an eternal youth."

"Reverend Beecher, I'm sorry to say this, but, as a man of science, I find it hard to believe that this operation will give you eternal youth."

"It is my heart's desire. And, mind you, it is not a selfish one. I only dream of it for the sake of salvaging this great country from ruin."

The Reverend Beecher talked about his great work of recanting his original abolitionist views. "I shall convince the North to remedy its mistakes and save the country," he said.

We listened to Beecher talk on an on for what seemed like an hour until Doctor Bell interrupted. "Sir, we must be on our way. May we now return to the topic of your operation?"

"Yes, of course. I am sorry, but politics have become my new religion, so to speak. My doctors have assured me that my ill health is due to a lack of glandular secretions. The injections I've been receiving are not helpful, so the next necessary step is a surgical implantation of tissue directly into my body."

"What is the origin of the glandular extracts?" Dr. Bell asked.

"I presume they are of animal origin."

"I agree that the Swiss have had some limited success with glandular implants, but only in very specific conditions of proven deficit."

"According to Dr. Droussard, the surgical incision is the only danger. He is willing to do the operation, but you are one of the world's best surgeons and use the new antiseptic technique. I trust there will be little risk and it would be my pleasure to have Mr. Doyle give the anaesthetic."

Dr. Bell's interest quickened at the name Droussard. "I insist on having my entire team, and I must inspect the local hospital facilities."

"It must be done in absolute secrecy. My doctors conduct experiments in a perfectly modern laboratory with suitable facilities for surgery," said the Reverend.

That was the end of the consultation. We left the stately mansion without a single glimpse of Rebecca.

It was a pleasant Tennessee day. The air was cool and crisp as we walked to the docks. Our vessel was eighteen feet long with four oars, a mast, sail, and tiller.

We set off downriver in high spirits. Carl and I each took a pair of oars. Rufus was at the stern with the tiller. Dr. Bell lounged on the bow seat and scanned the shores with a powerful telescope. A contrary southerly breeze precluded use of the sail, but with the strong current we made rapid progress.

After leaving Memphis the shoreline became low with innumerable small creeks and inlets. Dr. Bell pointed out hawks, shorebirds, turtles sunning on logs, otters, and even a black bear on the shore. It was a little after three o'clock in the afternoon when we rounded a bend and saw before us a small heavily wooded island and, much to our surprise, a two-story house—painted a bright scarlet-red.

We shipped our oars and drifted another quarter of a mile while Dr. Bell minutely surveyed the island. He passed the handsome brass instrument to me, and, after adjusting the lens, I examined the island, commencing with the scarlet house and the surrounding scarlet cabins.

The main building appeared to be an old-style Southern plantation house, and the cabins were probably slave quarters. There was no sign of human occupancy, but, over the door, outlined in black, was a flag. And it was not an old worn flag. It was new and bright red, with a blue cross and three white stars in each arm of the cross.

The rest of the island was densely covered with vegetation, right down to the water. I passed the telescope to Carl. "It's a Confederate battle flag," he said.

"Lemme see," said Rufus. He took a long look through the telescope. "Dat ain't just any Confederate battle flag."

When he passed the instrument back to me his hands shook. "Dat dere is the flag of old General Forrest. I told you this was a bad place."

We had drifted to within two hundred yards of the north end of the island when I heard a loud series of booms. Dr. Bell fell to his knees. "Gentlemen, get down!" he cried.

Rufus, Carl, and I all followed Dr. Bell's lead and dropped down to the deck. We heard a high-pitched noise as a volley of bullets whistled over our heads and splashed into the water on either side of the boat. I could see little puffs of gun smoke coming up from the edge of the island, but our assailant was well-hidden.

Dr. Bell coolly scanned the shore. "Whoever is shooting at us isn't visible, but he's no ghost. Gentlemen, please pull hard. We need to get out of range."

Carl went to his seat and pulled an oar to turn the boat. In my desperate attempt to duck from the bullets, I skimmed the water with my oars and fell backwards.

Carl managed to turn us towards the middle of the river and I thought we were safe. That is, until a few moments later when we were caught in an eddy current. The violent whirlpool spun our craft like a merry-go-round, further and further into the middle of the mighty river.

Suddenly, Dr. Bell grabbed my oar from me and his expert rowing brought us to the edge of the eddy. "I didn't know you knew how to row, sir," I said.

"Doyle, my lad, to you I might appear to be an old fogey, but, in my youth, I happened to have been the single scull champion of Edinb—"

Before he could finish his sentence, a final furious current took us back towards the island where we were greeted by another volley of rifle fire. A bullet smashed into a plank just at the water line of our boat. Instantly water poured in and we sank lower.

Dr. Bell and I kept rowing as Rufus and Carl tried to plug the bullet hole. Water poured in. Rufus desperately bailed with his hat while Carl cupped his hands and threw water overboard. Despite their best efforts, the boat settled deeper and deeper into the water.

We could not land on the island and the other shore was too far for us to reach before the boat sank. It looked hopeless. "Sir, any ideas on how we should proceed?" I asked.

"Stay with the boat, laddies, and have faith that this too shall pass!" Dr. Bell shouted.

We were down to the gunwales, frantically bailing with our cupped hands and hats when a low mournful wail rang in our ears. A steamboat was coming our way, a lovely grand vessel traveling upriver at a great speed. Her stern wheel chunked away; black smoke and sparks flew from her twin stacks into the rapidly darkening night.

She did not slow as we waved and shouted. No one on board saw us. To make matters worse, it appeared as if she was going to blindly ram our sinking vessel. Rufus and Carl pulled furiously on their oars. We narrowly escaped being rammed, but the boat had filled with water.

"I cain't swim!" Rufus shouted.

"Hang on to the boat!" Bell replied.

Suddenly, from behind the steamer, a small boat rowed by two powerful deckhands came our way. With extraordinary timing they arrived just as our boat was about to sink beneath the waves of old muddy. Our poor cockle shell was just barely afloat when our rescuers pulled us onto their little skiff and brought us to the steamer.

Within minutes, we were safely aboard the steamboat, *Natchez*, which was bound from Vicksburg to Memphis. The crew escorted us, dripping wet, through the grand ballroom, with a band and dancing couples, to the officer's quarters.

In all of America, I never saw anything as grand as that Mississippi River steamboat. The gilded decorations, gorgeous furniture, oil paintings, splendid food, abundant drinks, and hand-carved gambling tables took my breath away. She was a glorious embodiment of this young nation. Bold. Brash. Full of steam and power and energy.

Maybe it was our narrow escape from danger that filled us with a certain euphoria, or maybe it was the hot New Orleans coffee fortified with some sort of sweet, syrupy fluid that they served us as we were wrapped in warm blankets. Either way, it was as if we were snatched out of hell and carried into a heavenly abode. I will never forget those several glorious hours we spent on the *Natchez*.

By the time we docked in Memphis we were dry and warm. Dr. Bell seemed most bothered by the fact that the tobacco for his meerschaum pipe was a soggy mess. People often wonder why doctors are so addicted to this vile weed, but they need only endure the stench of an anatomy laboratory to understand.

"Doctor Bell, I would be happy to fetch pipe tobacco and pick up an El Perfecto cigar for myself," Carl said, with his usual good nature.

"Carl, I appreciate the offer, but it's getting late. You and Arthur should get some rest."

"I don't mind and would enjoy stopping by Angie's for a hot bowl of stew," said Carl.

"Do you want stew or that little blonde?" I teased.

Carl laughed. "The stew."

"Only if Arthur goes with you."

"This has been a most eventful day. I am exhausted and feel I must record everything in my diary before going to sleep," I insisted.

"I don't mind going alone. I'll only be an hour. I'll run to the tobacconist and then Angie's and be at the hotel in no time."

"No Carl, please, it may not be safe," Dr. Bell said.

Carl smiled, turned, and began running off into town.

"Doyle go after him!" Dr. Bell admonished me. "Rufus, please go with him. It is dangerous, too dangerous for any of you to be out alone. I will go to the hotel and wait there."

We did as he said, but, by the time we got started, Carl had gotten a good lead on us. In a near panic, we searched the streets and alleyways. He was nowhere to be found. We went to the tobacco shop. It was closed. A loud party was in progress at Angie's. I slipped around to the back door. "I ain't seen hide nor hair of Mister Carl," Ma said.

After searching for over an hour, not knowing where else we could look, we gave up and went back to the hotel.

When we returned Carl had still not appeared, but Dr. Bell was waiting in the lobby with a letter in hand.

My Dearest Dr. Bell,

My carriage will meet you at the hotel nine a.m., to-morrow. The operation we discussed will take place at noon, when there is the best light. I look forward to seeing you then and thank you for your assistance in advance.

Your Most Humble and Obedient Servant,

The Reverend Henry Ward Beecher

7 December, 1878

In the wee hours of the morning, I had a bad dream and awoke, certain that Carl would be snoring in the next bed. But, when I looked around the room, there was no sign of him. My nagging fears for his safety turned into a sinking sensation. Was he in the clutches of those evil people? Paralyzed and near death from curare? I ran to Dr. Bell's room and banged on the door. There was no answer.

I found Dr. Bell in the lobby pacing back and forth, empty pipe in hand.

"I should never have let him go after that damn bloody tobacco," he said. "I notified the police and sent a wire to Angus Duncan requesting assistance from the Pinkertons."

We again prowled the streets and alleys and visited Angie's. There was no sign of my friend, the best of America: an optimist and a trustworthy Wisconsin farm lad. Carl always had a smile on his face and never let anything oppress him. He had led me out of a freezing forest and saved my life more than once. I wondered where he could be and whether he was safe.

By nine o'clock in the morning, we were a dispirited group, waiting in the lobby for the Reverend Beecher. I was for putting the whole thing off until we found Carl, but Dr. Bell grimly observed that in all likelihood the minister would lead us to the fiends who had abducted Carl. The carriage arrived, but I was too distraught to pay attention to the two armed horsemen who followed the Reverend Beecher.

To my surprise, Rebecca was sitting next to the minister. *What a cozy arrangement*, I thought. We settled ourselves on the opposite seat, leaving room for Rufus who carried the instrument case. The Reverend's face twisted into a smirk. "Is his presence necessary, Doctor Bell?" he asked.

"Aye, absolutely. Mr. Freeman is an integral member of my surgical team. Your operation cannot proceed without him," Dr. Bell replied.

Rebecca's eyes were downcast. She did not meet my gaze. "Jimmy is almost back to his normal self," she murmured.

I leaned across the narrow space that separated us. "That's good. How are you?"

"Happy because now I shall have time to nurse the Reverend Beecher after his operation."

"I see." I turned from her and gazed out the window.

"Arthur, where is your friend, Carl? I thought for sure that he would be here to assist in the operation," she asked.

"He's gone missing," I said.

"Oh, I am so sorry. I had hoped to see him again. I hope he will be all right."

To my great consternation, Rebecca spent her time arranging pillows or tucking the minister's feet under blankets. Every so often I glanced at her, hoping that she might be looking at me. But, it was as if I never existed.

We galloped in a southerly direction, past fields left fallow for the winter, then through dense woodland and swamps, for at least an hour. We stopped by a trail that led through a desolate, forbidding swamp.

It was then that I noticed the two silent men who had followed us on horseback. They and our driver held Winchester rifles. One man led the way on the trail beneath dark, low-hanging clouds. The rain started with a drizzle, but quickly became a downpour before we reached the waiting steam launch. We huddled in the shelter of the small deckhouse as we chugged downstream past ancient trees hung with a greyish moss. I moved as close as possible to Rebecca, who was hunched in a corner.

She said nothing, but, to my surprise, she took my hand as if she were searching for comfort or reassurance. My heart did a flip-flop, but, in a moment, she removed her hand and silently moved closer to the Reverend Beecher.

Our vessel touched ground, and, while balancing on a narrow gangplank that ended in a muddy path, a great flash of lightning revealed the scarlet house and surrounding cabins on top of the small hill. We were on the back side of the island. Evidently the river continued around the southern edge to join the Mississippi.

Our silent guards cradled polished new Winchester rifles in the crook of their arms. "Why are you armed?" Dr. Bell asked.

"Damned dangerous in these parts. Alligators and rattlesnakes and the like," one replied, as he spit a stream of tobacco juice.

We were walking up a muddy path when I spotted a crumpled, soggy El Perfecto cigar, Carl's favourite smoke, beside the path. I had the wild hope that we would find him alive. As we trudged up the path through driving rain towards the scarlet house I heard chattering, howling, and crying. It was as if the house had a nursery filled with babies who were making an eerie, almost inhuman sound. The rogue at the head of our column bought his rifle to his shoulder and scanned the trees on either side of the path.

Rufus, for all his superstitions, seemed the least concerned about our surroundings. He proudly carried the instrument case at the head of our dreary column. Dr. Bell kept a grim silence and stolidly treaded onward. I caught up with him to gain strength from his resolve. There was no chance to tell him about the cigar because the Reverend Beecher insisted on stopping to catch his breath. "Don't waste our time. Get along," one of the armed men said.

"I understand the need for secrecy since I am destined to be the next President of the United States, but I demand an explanation for the guns," said the Reverend Beecher with an angry scowl.

There was no answer because the Reverend Beecher took a feeble step, slipped on a stone, and went down. Rebecca helped him to his feet and on we went.

We finally reached the scarlet plantation house and the howling and chattering reached an otherworldly pitch and then died out . . .

It had once been a grand mansion, but now the columns were askew and most of the floor boards on the veranda were rotting.

One of our keepers shifted his Winchester and, with a large key, unlocked the front door beneath the painted battle flag. We stepped into a long corridor containing odd pieces of once-elegant furniture. It ran the length of the front of the house, and by the light of oil lamps I identified four doors leading off the corridor. The chattering and crying, which had ceased when we entered the corridor, started back again, this time with greater intensity and a note of madness and anger.

To my amazement, the door to our left opened into a clean whitewashed room. Rain beat against a skylight that admitted light the color of cast iron. Oil lamps helped relieve the gloom.

There was a plain wooden operating table in the center of the room beneath the skylight. Shelves filled with medical supplies lined the walls. Next to the operating table was a small table with a wash basin, soap, and towels. The room was heated by an old-fashioned open fireplace.

My eyes swept across what was to be our operating room. In addition to the entrance, there was another closed door. Did it lead to another room or to the outside? A tall, stooped woman clad in the white floor-length dress of a proper operating room sister was in charge. A bonnet pulled low obscured her hair and features. Upon our arrival, she ceased stacking linen on a shelf and half turned with a folded towel over her right hand.

"The table is freshly scrubbed and prepared for the Reverend Beecher. You may place the instruments there." She pointed to another table covered with a white sheet. "I trust everything is satisfactory."

Dr. Bell swept the room with his eyes. "Aye, the room seems well-organized, but where is the Reverend Beecher's physician?"

"Dr. Droussard will be here after he secures the glandular material."

"I understand the desire for secrecy, but why have we been threatened with firearms?"

"Our men are armed to discourage trespassers and to protect you from wild animals. We are quite removed from civilization."

Dr. Bell nodded to Rufus who placed the instrument case on the edge of the table. The minister, holding Rebecca's arm, tottered into the operating room. He removed his coat and shirt and, almost eagerly, stretched out on the table.

"Prepare both arms, please. The doctor may implant two glands," said the nurse.

Rufus soaked the instruments in carbolic and Rebecca, at Dr. Bell's instructions, swabbed both of the Reverend Beecher's arms with the antiseptic.

Dr. Bell was quiet and pensive. His interest in the operation appeared to be as much curiosity as scientific interest.

The preparations for surgery proceeded normally until Dr. Bell instructed Mr. Freeman to give the chloroform and Miss Yates to handle the instruments. I would normally have given the anaesthetic, but assumed he was giving Mr. Freeman the experience because this operation was a mere incision through the skin and fat.

The wild chattering and raucous noise had died down. I became aware of a low moaning, almost gurgling, sound from the back room. Fearing the worst, I could not help but creep towards the closed door. While everyone concentrated on the Reverend Beecher, I quietly inched opened the door.

Suddenly, large, rough, powerful hands grabbed me by the shoulders and covered my mouth, stifling my outcry. The door was closed and I was overpowered and forced to the ground. It happened so quickly, I was afraid that my companions, busy with their preparations, were unaware of my predicament and would not notice my disappearance.

As I struggled against my assailants to get to my feet, I felt a slight stabbing sensation in my right buttock. A moment later I lost voluntary motion, first in my legs, then my arms. I was still perfectly aware of my surroundings, with unimpaired vision and hearing. However, when they roughly placed me on a table, I realized I was no longer able to hold up my head.

With my death likely imminent from suffocation, I remembered Dr. Bell's advice to breathe with the diaphragm, the muscle that separates the abdomen from the chest cavity. I concentrated every fiber of my being on the phrenic nerve that innervates the diaphragm.

But, I could not budge my diaphragm. My chest felt heavy and dead. I was going to be asphyxiated. I wanted to scream. I wanted to breathe.

I did not want to die.

I focused all my mental energy on my phrenic nerve until there was a flicker of movement. I felt a minute flow of air enter my lungs. I flexed my diaphragm again and again in an attempt to maintain a tenuous hold on life.

I heard a low gurgling together with a constant trickling sound that, at first, I thought was water. To my horror, it was the drip, drip, drip of blood.

They had left me with my head turned to one side, and as my vision cleared, I looked upon a dreadfully horrific scene.

Carl, my best mate in America, was naked from the waist up and strapped to a table. A gowned, hooded figure held back his head while another, similarly attired, dissected with knife and forceps deep into a bloody hole in his neck.

The paralyzing drug that they had given us both still had me in its hold, but Carl started to squirm as they probed his neck in an attempt to remove his thyroid gland.

Suddenly, Carl jerked and attempted to struggle free. He moaned and his eyes rolled towards me with a startled look of recognition.

I wanted to reach out to help him, to do something, but I was incapable of movement.

The surgeon, or rather I should call him the detestable butcher posing as a surgeon, continued with painstaking slowness to dissect through the nerves, blood vessels and muscles of Carl's neck.

There was a steady drip of blood, and occasionally a crimson spray when the sharp knife cut through an artery.

I willed my paralyzed muscles to stir, but could not force even the merest twitch of movement. I felt a constant sensation of suffocation, as if I was being held under water by a giant hand and could not rise to the surface. I felt lucky to occasionally get a tiny gasp of air into my lungs.

I momentarily went unconscious from lack of oxygen, but something—call it a deep-seated atavistic need to survive—forced the diaphragmatic muscle to quiver now and move the merest whiffs of air into my body.

The high-pitched chattering increased. Something banged and knocked at a side door. The surgeon continued slowly dissecting Carl's neck.

I drifted in and out of consciousness while the operation on Carl proceeded step by agonizing step. I had no sensation of the passage of time, but concentrated on each shallow breath. Carl's moans and gurgling respirations became weaker until, with one final gasp, his beseeching eyes turned to me. *Kill me. Now. Please*, they seemed to plead.

His life's blood drained out onto the floor and I knew he was knocking on death's door. My foggy, oxygen-starved brain understood. They were not implanting glands into the Reverend Beecher from animals, but from human beings. They had kidnapped Carl to implant his thyroid into the Reverend to re-invigorate him. It was a hideous, detestable plan.

But, yes, now I understood. The nurse had said they would implant two glands. I was to be the next subject.

Rough hands straightened my body into a supine position and tilted my head backwards to expose the flesh of my neck to the surgeon's knife.

The memory of the scene that followed is both a confused blur and a vivid nightmare.

The chattering increased to a frenzied howl, and the door on the opposite side of the room swung open. A horde of screeching and howling monkeys flew out through the door and descended on the hooded figures ripping, clawing, and biting.

The surgeon and the medical assistant attempted to defend themselves with surgical knives, but the frenzied animals tore away their hoods and robes and overcame them.

Suddenly, a small woman's body with long, flowing locks of raven hair passed before my eyes, and I realized that the surgeon was none other than Emilie Droussard. She covered her face with her hands to protect herself, but the animals were not deterred. They ripped her skin and bit deep into her neck, chest, and head. Blood spewed everywhere.

She screamed as they bore her down to the floor. Her blood mingled with Carl's. She struggled against the mad primate onslaught for another moment and then, mercifully for her, she passed out.

One large, fierce monkey fastened on to the back of her assistant who I now realized was the tobacco-spitting man with the Winchester rifle who had walked us to the scarlet house.

The man beat the animal with his bare hands and struck it with the butt of his rifle, but to no avail. As he staggered from their onslaught, his arms flailing furiously, two monkeys shredded his face with their razor-sharp incisor teeth.

As if possessed by demons, the ferocious monkeys tore his eyes from their sockets. He emitted an unholy scream and sunk, lifeless, to the floor.

Throughout this ghastly uproar, I fully expected the monkeys to attack me and Carl. We were helpless and the next victims.

A monkey even jumped onto my chest, but, instead of ripping me to pieces, to my amazement, it merely sniffed and jumped down.

Suddenly, the once-ferocious monkeys became docile as family pets and scampered about, ignoring the bodies and lapping up human blood.

Two of the animals leaped up on to the surgical table, sniffed Carl, and made sad, mewing sounds. Carl stirred. He was still alive! My heart leaped with joy.

However, his chest hardly moved, and I was certain that, without medical attention, he would surely die.

It all made sense when I dimly remembered surgical scars on the monkeys. These simple primates had been subject to dreadful experiments, yet, somehow, they had survived. Now, they had taken revenge on their tormenters.

Suddenly, the room went grey, then black. Dr. Bell later said my eyes were wide open, but I was unconscious when he and Rebecca burst into the room.

They heard the ruckus and, fortunately, arrived just in time. Rebecca thought I was dead and, with quick thinking, grabbed the bellows from the fireplace. "Dr. Bell, he isn't breathing!" she shouted.

Dr. Bell immediately pumped air into my lungs. They said I initially showed no signs of life.

At the first twinge of returning muscle activity, I weakly brushed the wooden nozzle away from my mouth, coughed, spluttered, and took a deep breath. "Save Carl," I said.

Poor Carl was near the end of his life, but if there was one man in the world who could save him it was Dr. Joseph Bell.

"Aye, he has a faint pulse!" Dr. Bell shouted. "Miss Yates, please, my instruments . . ."

Rebecca snatched up clamps, needles, and thread. In the merest twinkling of an eye, Dr. Bell sutured bleeding arteries and veins. The bleeding stopped. Dr. Bell had trained in the old days before anaesthetics, when surgeons operated with great speed. His fingers flew, and it was only minutes until he had stitched the terrible wound.

In the midst of the frantic efforts to stitch the wound, Carl had stopped breathing. Dr. Bell responded to this new emergency and pumped air into his lungs with the fireplace bellows. Carl did not respond. Dr. Bell, a staunch churchman, looked to heaven, and I am certain his lips moved in prayer, entreating God for a miracle.

Dr. Bell kept pumping the bellows. Suddenly, Carl took a weak breath, coughed, sputtered, and came back to life. To our great joy, he was alive.

If the monkeys had come a minute later, Carl would've been dead, and if Dr. Bell and Rebecca hadn't arrived shortly after the monkey attack, I would've been dead, too. Yet, it was as if some sort of divine force had wanted us to survive and so, we were both saved.

(I do not remember a great deal about my rescue. Therefore, I must admit that the details as written were related to me by Rebecca and Dr. Bell after these events took place. They also told of the events as they transpired in the adjoining room of the scarlet house in the few minutes before my rescue. Ergo, the following text is his tale as they related it to me after it occurred.)

Doctor Bell, with his usual way, dictated the following between puffs on his pipe: *I was focused on the operation, dubious, yet I must admit, also excited about, the possibilities of a great scientific breakthrough. Lister's antiseptic technique made it possible to remove or repair diseased organs. If this operation succeeded, organ implantation could become a reality.*

Rufus had administered sufficient chloroform and the nursing sister indicated the organ was nearly ready in the adjacent room. I had made a mere scratch of an incision on the Reverend Beecher's right arm. "Doyle, please finish the incision down to muscle. You need the practise," I said.

When you did not respond, I looked around and realized that you, laddie, had disappeared. I put down the scalpel and demanded to know your whereabouts.

The nursing sister insisted that I continue with the operation. I expressed concern and adamantly refused until she revealed your whereabouts.

As I looked at the nursing sister, I observed something. You see, my dear Doyle, once again, it was observation that saved the day...

For the nursing sister was no woman.

I tore off her white bonnet and flung aside the towel covering the right hand only to reveal an awful hook. As you may now have guessed, the nursing sister was really Captain Spencer or, as he is better known, Captain Hook.

The villain jumped away from me. He seized Rebecca just beneath her jaw with his terribly sharp hook and, with his good hand, pulled a long-barrelled revolver from beneath his white dress. His face was contorted with rage and he had the strength of a mad man.

I immediately poised the scalpel over Beecher's chest.

"Damn you! I shall plunge this knife into his heart. Release the girl."

He was far gone into madness, but Rufus flung himself at the Captain. The man fired his pistol, but the gun caught on his long dress. His aim was poor. The bullet grazed Rufus on the side of his chest. The ragged wound was bloody and painful, but not lethal.

Just before he collapsed, Rufus seized the weapon. Thankfully, the open instrument case was close at hand. I reached into my secret niche and withdrew the Bull Dog revolver.

My first shot splintered the doorway. I aimed again, but Hook used Rebecca as a shield and I lowered the gun.

(Here, Miss Yates took up the narrative. She spoke in a low, almost inaudible voice, while twisting a handkerchief. She was clearly under great emotional strain as she spoke, but I felt it important to convey her story in order to complete this narrative.)

It all happened so fast. He dragged me backwards and said he would kill me if Doctor Bell didn't continue the operation. I felt helpless and terrified as the cold metal of his hook dug into my throat.

With his last ounce of strength, heroic Rufus pushed him off balance and took his gun. When Doctor Bell fired, I wrenched free. He then fled down the corridor, tearing off the dress as he ran. In his flight, he knocked over an oil lamp. Oil *spilled and burst into flames. The fire spread through the old furniture and dry wood. He reached the front door and disappeared. "Down with tyrants!" he screamed.*

(Dr. Bell took up the narrative again here.)

When I reached Rebecca, the corridor was already filled with black smoke and flames were licking at the walls. Captain Hook had disappeared, but a door at the end of the hall opened and a man holding a rifle and a whip stepped out.

When I fired, he ran and disappeared around the corner, apparently following Captain Hook into the approaching night.

To my amazement and utter horror, a pack of shrieking monkeys emerged from the door and ran through the flames and smoke. They ignored us and scampered out of the house.

After I had seen to Rebecca and staunched the bleeding from Rufus's chest I then proceeded to help you and Carl.

(I shall now continue the narrative from my own perspective.)

As Carl and I began to recover, Dr. Bell and Rebecca dragged Rufus into our 'operating room'. They then pulled the Reverend Beecher from the approaching flames. He was still recovering from the anaesthetic. They slammed the door behind them, but the smoke poured in through the cracks around the doorstop.

Flames were rapidly consuming the house, smoke was filling our room, and we could not see a way out. A quick inspection of the 'operating room' revealed the windows were barred on the outside and there was no other door.

We considered making a *run* through the flames to an exit, but the floorboards started collapsing, and we seemed destined to die of asphyxiation in this ghastly room in this gruesome scarlet house.

A few feet away from me, suddenly I heard Emilie Droussard. "Dr. Bell . . . Please . . ." She slowly raised her bloody arm and pointed to a shelf.

Dr. Bell knelt by her side and listened to her nearly inaudible, wispy voice "It was a mad dream . . . My casebook . . . Take it. You will see . . ."

Her arm fell back and her eyes closed. She made a deep shuddering sigh. Her eyes fluttered open, "If only . . . The implant . . ." Her voice drifted off, and then her eyes brightened for an instant. "To hays . . . Below the tomb!"

She said nothing more, but took another raspy breath. Her eyes went dim with the blank emptiness of death. Dr. Bell then reached for her casebook, a leather-bound notebook sitting on an overhead shelf. Dr. Bell slipped it into his coat pocket.

Rufus groaned in pain and Dr. Bell tried to assist him.

Meanwhile, the smoke continued to fill the room, and Rebecca was the first to succumb to the fumes. She slumped and fell to the floor. She struck the hard wooden floorboards with a loud *FWUNK*. I was dizzy and still badly shaken, but knelt by her side, fanning her face and massaging her hands. I coughed and wondered how much longer we could survive the smoke and flames.

Things looked grim. The smoke was growing thick. We were lost.

"Doyle, how is Rebecca?" Doyle shouted through the haze of smoke.

"Her pulse is steady and her breath is shallow."

Rebecca opened her eyes. "What happened?"

"You fainted."

"Doyle, did you hear the hollow sound as she hit the floor? It sounded hollow. Please inspect the floorboards!" Dr. Bell yelled.

The smoke made it hard to see, but I ran my hands along the floorboards by Rebecca. I noticed nothing unusual. The floorboards were old and worn.

Just as I was about to give up, my hand struck upon something cold and metallic. Brass. There was a round, tarnished brass door-pull set deeply into a plank in the floorboards.

"I found a trapdoor handle . . . You were right, Dr. Bell. How did you know?"

"Elementary. Did you not interpret the hollow sound as Rebecca fell?"

It was a trapdoor that led to a flight of stairs, then into a cavernous basement dug out of the earth and lined by crude bricks. Like priest-holes in old English homes, many pre-Civil War homes in America had trapdoors that led to tunnels. We were saved, thanks to Dr. Bell's great powers of observation.

Dr. Bell and I supported Rufus while we made our way down wet, moss covered wooden stairs into the dank subterranean room. The Reverend Beecher, now fully recovered from the chloroform, followed us. And Carl, my magnificently strong mate from Wisconsin, struggled to get to his feet. Unfortunately, he was still very weak and, as he tried to stand, he collapsed back to the floor.

Rebecca, poor, sweet Rebecca, felt better and helped Carl to his feet and down the stairs of the tunnel.

Once everybody was safely below the ground, I slammed the trapdoor against the dense smoke and breathed a sigh of relief. Dr. Bell gently lowered Rufus to the earthen floor and I struck a lucifer.

By the flickering yellow light we made out dozens of wooden crates labeled 'U.S. ARMORY, WINCHESTER CALIBRE .45-70 RIFLES.' Were these the guns stolen from an arsenal in Illinois? I had no time to ponder the question. It was pitch dark when my match went out.

I used up all but one match while exploring to find an exit. There was nothing. I pulled slivers of wood from a crate and, with my last match, created a makeshift torch.

I held the burning slivers high and explored more until I felt a slight draft of fresh air from a side tunnel leading down and away from the crude basement.

"Follow me." I went ahead with the dim torch and our motley parade trudged in the dark towards the draft of fresh air. Rebecca supported Carl and Dr. Bell helped Rufus. The Reverend Beecher complained at every step while we crept along the muddy tunnel. I may have stepped on a rat, but stifled a scream for fear of upsetting Rebecca. She cried out and batted at a spider web in her hair. The spider was a black, wicked-looking creature. I never liked creepy insects, but I brushed it away and stepped on it.

We had been in the tunnel no more than a few minutes when a terrific explosion shook the earth. Bricks flew from the walls and all around us the tunnel began to collapse.

"My God, there must have been enough powder and ammunition there for a small army," said Dr. Bell. "Hurry, before we are buried alive."

We moved as quickly as we could under the circumstances. Fortunately, we soon saw a speck of light, which grew larger as we moved closer to it. In a moment, we emerged into some brush only a few yards from the big river. The tunnel entrance was well-hidden by trees and foliage.

Muddy footprints in a worn trail leading to a crude landing indicated recent use.

I searched, but the steam launch that had brought us here was gone, most likely taken by Captain Hook and his rifle-toting crony.

Flames and dense smoke still shot skyward from the old scarlet plantation house and were spreading fast to the cabins. We watched as the house collapsed into a veritable crematorium for Emilie Droussard and her accomplices. Meanwhile, the storm moved on, leaving a yellow haze that marked the sun setting across the great river.

About an hour later, a side-wheeler packet boat pushing a flat-bottomed barge had paused in mid-river, evidently to watch the spectacular pyrotechnics. We shouted and waved. Finally, Dr. Bell fired three quick shots from his Bull Dog revolver.

The Reverend Beecher finally proved of some value when he shouted in his best stentorian voice. "HELP! HELP! We have injured men here!"

She was the *Lucy B*, an elderly tug pushing a barge upriver. Her great wheel churned mud, but she edged close enough to our landing for husky black deckhands to help us aboard.

On board, we huddled among bales of cotton, trying to make Carl and Rufus comfortable. Carl had lost a lot of blood and had used all of his remaining energy to get through the tunnel. He was pale and weak as he rested on the cotton bales.

Rufus coughed and spit blood as if the bullet had grazed his lung. More blood oozed from his chest wound. Fortunately, the bullet had entered his lower chest and exited from his side. Dr. Bell swabbed his wounds with carbolic and applied a tight bandage torn from his shirt.

Rebecca, now fully revived from inhaling smoke, took over his care with great tenderness. The five of us huddled together and sat away from the Reverend Beecher. The old fellow was angry that we had not implanted the thyroid gland. He was still convinced the operation would have made him into a new man. Even now, he could not believe that his doctor was a fraud.

We reached the Memphis landing a few hours later and, with difficulty, roused a drayman and his wagon.

With my energy somewhat restored by the fresh air, I went ahead and informed the Burk's of our plight. They were more than willing to take in my injured companions and tend to their needs. Upon arrival at the Burk's house, Rebecca, Dr. Bell, and I carried Rufus and then Carl into the home of the friendly Quakers.

Rebecca shook her red curls. "I shall have nothing more to do with the Reverend Beecher. Please, Mrs. Burk, I have a little money and will pay if you can let my ward, Jimmy, stay with you for a few days while I care for these two injured men." Her eyes flashed with an emotion that I had never witnessed in the girl.

"Of course, dear, you may stay as long as you wish."

So, Miss Yates stayed with Rufus and Carl.

Soon thereafter Dr. Bell and I retired to the hotel where I am once again at my desk with pencil and paper recording the events of this incredible day. I am at this moment reading out loud to Dr. Bell, who is kindly correcting some of my observations. To the best of my memory it is all true. I am glad to be alive and looking forward to spending the remainder of my time in America wooing Rebecca. How can I ever thank Doctor Bell for saving my life? Someday, I shall immortalize this man with my writing.

8 December, 1878

In the morning, after a sound sleep, Dr. Bell and I picked up Jimmy from the Payne's mansion and delivered him to the Burk's house.

On the way, I asked Dr. Bell about the Reverend. Beecher. "You need not worry about that old scoundrel. The sly old dog slithered back to Brooklyn on the first train. The old fraud tried to swear me to secrecy before he left and said he would pray for us."

We brought young Jimmy and all of his and Rebecca's luggage to the Burk's home. Rufus and Carl were on makeshift pallets in our old lean-to bedroom. Their wounds were clean, but both patients were in considerable pain. When we arrived with Jimmy, Miss Yates was administering laudanum to Carl. My friend gazed at her with what were clearly love-smitten eyes and, when she put down the bottle of medicine, she caressed his hand and returned his loving gaze. Was it possible? Had they fallen in love overnight?

Rebecca rose, hugged little Jimmy and then gave me a mere glance. "Mrs. Burk will allow me to stay as long as it takes to restore Carl and Rufus to health," said she. She smiled warmly as she spoke. In that moment, a spark flashed between Rebecca and Carl and I knew that they had taken a fancy to each other.

Despite all my efforts to woo her, she had instead fallen for my friend from Wisconsin, and he was just as smitten.

I must admit, as I watched them stare deeply into each other's eyes, I did feel the sharp stab of green-eyed jealousy. Our star-crossed love was not to be. At first I was angry, but then I felt happy for my mate, Carl. It was a struggle, but I became resigned to focusing on the other dreams in my life: finishing my studies, learning medicine, and, someday, writing about my adventures in America. Even with a broken heart, I would wish them well. She was the pretty nurse that Carl had longed for. Perhaps the prophecy of Mrs. Burk's tea leaves was correct and marrying her would have upset my Maw. My scientific mind would not accept the occult, but perhaps there are unknown mysteries.

Aye, it is disappointing and hard to accept. Surely, there has to be someone else out there for me. Somebody who wants me as much as I want them. I am still only nineteen and have the rest of my life to learn the ways of women.

Back in the kitchen, over cups of Mrs. Burk's coffee, Dr. Bell lit up his pipe. "I wish I could say all's well that ends well, but, alas, we still aren't free to return to Scotland."

"Why?" I asked.

"Our friend, Captain Hook is still at large."

"Aye, but he is no threat."

"Doyle, my lad, do you remember Emilie Droussard's dying words?"

"Something about 'to hays below the tomb.' "

"Something bad is afoot, but I am baffled."

Rufus overheard our conversation and weakly lifted his head from the pallet. "Sir, dey's only one tomb important to those damn Confederates. The good folks up North buried Mister Lincoln in a fine tomb in Springfield, Illinois."

Dr. Bell nodded. "They might steal the body, but that would not further their cause. Hmmm . . . Let me ponder this. Doyle, let us take a walk. The fresh air might help."

It was a sunny, fine day with just a bit of a breeze. We strolled back to the Peabody for lunch, and as is his habit, Dr. Bell stopped in the lobby to check the newspapers.

"My God. Doyle, read this." I took the paper and scanned a long article on the front page about the travels of President Rutherford B. Hayes from Washington, through the Midwest to Kansas, and back through Springfield, Illinois. The President was to end his tour with a final address at Lincoln's tomb at four o'clock in the afternoon on the ninth day of December.

I gasped. "That was her message. Not to hays, but to Rutherford B. HAYES."

"Aye and BELOW the tomb. President Hayes will be delivering a speech on the balustrade BELOW the obelisk marking Lincoln's tomb, and he very well might share Lincoln's fate if we do not intercede by four o'clock in the afternoon to-morrow," said Dr. Bell.

TO-MORROW! The President was going to be in Springfield in one day. We had to get there if we were to stop something awful from happening.

"Get a cab! We must warn Angus at once!" Dr. Bell shouted.

I hailed the first cab. Dr. Bell offered the driver a gold eagle to reach the central depot and the telegraph office within five minutes. The driver whipped his horse to a furious gallop. By his gold watch, the time was four minutes later when we reached the depot.

Dr. Bell presented his scribbled message to the operator, an obese gentleman with a flowing white beard dotted with brown dribbles of tobacco juice.

"Please send this urgent message to Mr. Angus Duncan in Chicago," Dr. Bell said. The message read: *Alert the Pinkertons. Potential tragedy to occur to-morrow at Lincoln's tomb at four o'clock in the afternoon. Must be stopped.*

The operator chewed his gob of tobacco while reading the message, paused for a moment, then aimed a stream of brown spit at Dr. Bell's feet. "You damn Yankees have done enough damage."

"I am a subject of her British majesty. A Scot, to be specific. Not a Yankee."

"If you ain't Southern, you're a damn Yankee in my book. I would be damned to hell before I send this message for you, even if I could. Big ice storm up North, all lines are down, bridges washed out, ain't even no trains runnin'."

"Please route the message to another line. I shall pay you in gold," said Dr. Bell.

"Hell, no."

"I shall call the police."

"Go ahead. They locked up the last carpetbaggers who came into town. Sure they would be happy to lock you up, too."

The operator was correct. No trains were running north. Dr. Bell consulted the station map. "It is over three hundred miles to Springfield. If we ride day and night we can make it in time."

I disagreed. "Doctor Bell, horses won't be able to get us there in time. Do you have any other ideas?"

"You are probably right. Well then, if we can ride these horses to Cairo, Illinois, we might be able to catch a train there."

We obtained two good horses and saddles and immediately set out at a gallop on the only road heading north. The first fifteen miles sped by, but our horses were tiring and my backside was already sore as a boil.

We were on the outskirts of a small town when we spied a crowd of men, lads, and women around some sort of show in an open field. As we drew closer we saw a hot air balloon being inflated.

"Whoa!" Dr. Bell shouted. "This demands investigation."

A portly man in a set of white overalls paced in front of the balloon on jerky steps while wringing his hands. "Ladies and Gents. Just one dollar a person for a full twenty-five minute ride in the world's largest hot air balloon . . . Boys, be the first to tell your friends you kissed your girl while five-hundred feet in the air."

A few young fellows scuffed their feet and looked interested, but no one opened their wallets. We drew closer to see a wicker basket connected to the balloon that was tethered to the ground with ropes. Above the basket, flames from a metal tank heated the air that inflated the balloon.

Dr. Bell inspected the contraption. "Sir, can your balloon go as far as Springfield, Illinois?"

"Well, well, well . . . Lookee here, lookee here . . . Hear that there accent, folks? Yes, they come all the way from England to ride Oscar's world famous balloon."

"We are from Scotland, not England," said I.

"Either way, you came to the right place, gents. Yes sir, it is your lucky day." He held a finger to the wind. "If this south wind holds, she could probably take you all the way back home to Wales."

"Scotland."

"And the fee, sir?" Dr. Bell asked.

"Since you gentlemen came all this way, I'll give you a special discount. Remember, this is the world's largest balloon and a once-in-a-lifetime opportunity. Take a ride! Take a death-defying ride and make history!" he said, as much to the crowd as to us.

"The fee, sir?" Dr. Bell asked once again.

"Because the British have been such great friends to these here colonies and you are so beloved, I shall give a special fee reserved customarily for family members. And gents, this fee will be a special offer, a never-to-be-repeated price, so if you don't grab it the instant I quote it—"

"PLEASE, just tell us the fee!"

"A mere one hundred dollars."

"That's highway robbery!" I yelled.

"I tell you, gents, and this is the God's honest truth, one hundred dollars for a chance to ride in the world's largest balloon is a steal. An unheard of, never-to-be-repeated deal. At that price, gents, you are robbing me."

Dr. Bell shook his head in disgust. "We shall give you the horses and saddles now, and twenty dollars upon arrival, if you can get us there by three o'clock to-morrow."

"DEAL. You gents drive a hard bargain. And please do not tell another soul about this special rate that I only give to friends from across the pond in merry old England." He extended his hand and shook Dr. Bell's. "The name's Oscar. Oscar Blithe. My balloon is named *Blithe Spirit*. Now, climb in the basket and off we go."

We introduced ourselves and climbed in. "Make haste, sir. We have no time to lose, and need to go as soon as possible," Dr. Bell urged.

"As you wish. We'll be off in a moment. Just need to turn up the heat."

The balloon itself was constructed of panels of red, white, and blue silk. The gas tank, suspended just within reach above the basket, was equipped with a valve to control the flow of gas, and a flint and steel igniter that made a spark when the operator pulled a string.

After we crowded into the basket Mr. Blithe opened a valve. Blue flames shot upward sending hot air into the balloon. The great silken bag inflated and tugged at its mooring line. "Let her go!" Oscar shouted.

We hauled in the ropes and we were up and away.

When we were high over the tree tops, Oscar shut off the gas and we sailed through the sky in absolute silence. It was so perfectly peaceful, unlike anything I had known. I felt tension and worry draining away. Happily, I had brought my diary and a pencil with me so I could record the experience.

I was calm and tranquil for the first time in many days. The sighing wind and clear skies were a balm to my soul. It was utter serenity—that is until Oscar broke into my thoughts.

"You folks are in for a real treat. It's a clear sunny day and you can see forever. We're following the river to Cairo. Then, if the wind holds, we will strike a compass course to Springfield." Oscar stated this with so much enthusiasm that I was convinced we would reach Springfield in plenty of time.

At one point, Oscar gave up on his travelogue and began fussing with the gas burner. My gaze rested upon the great river, which twisted and turned for miles and miles like an endless serpent. There were sandbars, shores lined with greeny-grey trees, and a few villages hugging the river banks. Steamboats glided along, belching clouds of dense black smoke.

I scarcely had words to describe the magnificence of this land, which made me wonder if I could ever really be a good enough writer to share my adventures with the world.

This was the first time I truly had the opportunity to study Dr. Bell in repose. He had removed his great cape and the wool hat with earflaps that so effectively repels the icy, whistling winds and drenching rains of our Scottish climate. His eyes were closed against the sun and he folded his hands over chest. I could not help but sketch his aquiline profile and jutting jaw to fasten that moment in my memory.

The wind was starting to die, which meant our speed diminished. Dr. Bell came instantly awake, reached for his great curved pipe, tamped in tobacco, lit up and watched the smoke drift skyward.

"Mr. Blithe, we are slowing. If you please, canna you make mair speed?" he asked, with a pronounced, rarely used Scottish burr.

"I'll give her some more gas. We'll get a better wind if we go higher up," Mr. Blithe said.

He opened the valve and pulled the igniter string again. Immediately, a blue flame roared out of the tank and the balloon lifted higher and then even higher.

We flew along as fast as a railway train, but Oscar said we were going no more than twenty-five miles an hour. Either way, I figured that we were going more than fast enough to get us to Springfield in time.

Riding in the balloon was a welcome, tranquil experience and a great relief after being shot at in Chicago, nearly hanged by the James Gang, almost drowned, poisoned by curare, scared half to death by vengeance-seeking monkeys, and losing Rebecca to my mate.

However, the placidity was occasionally broken by our balloonist. As we passed over a sizable village, farm, or town, Oscar waved and yelled 'hallo!' to folks gathered below. The people looked upward as if hearing a voice from heaven and then waved and hollered back. From our vantage point, they were as small as dolls. Oscar was a lively fellow and had evidently entertained guests before.

"Would you fellows care for a little snack or drink of homemade hooch?"

Oscar hoisted a jug and glugged down a half a cup of raw hooch.

"English balloonists serve champagne," said Dr. Bell.

I wolfed down a half-loaf of hard black bread and a moldy hunk of cheese cheddar. I even took a sip of Oscar's homebrew. Dr. Bell tipped up the jug for me and then helped himself to a long drink.

Dr. Bell touched his lips with a handkerchief. "Not up to a good Scottish malt, but, not bad, not bad. Mr. Blithe, we must not get behind our schedule. Please, make haste."

"Have no worries, my friends. I will have you in Springfield within the hour," Oscar responded.

Except for the wind and the occasional roar of the gas flame, it was once again tranquil. I rushed to write down my final thoughts because, surely, our adventure was soon to be over. Sadly, too, all was over with Rebecca. I searched for a word that could help me move on and the one that came to mind was *exorcise*. Yes, I would erase her from my thoughts and remember this grand landscape.

While I was writing we passed over a lake. With no warning a whirlwind struck the balloon. Suddenly, our basket was swinging madly, like a pendulum. I was forced to put aside my pencil and cling to a rope for dear life. The basket tipped, made a great splintering noise, and spun like a top. I was certain we would fall to our death. Dr. Bell, for all his fearlessness in the face of danger, was deathly pale.

Oscar remained his jovial self. "Ain't nothin', boys. Just warm air rising from that lake down under. Old *Blithe Spirit* has seen worse than this. Have some more whisky."

I held tight and felt the bread, cheese, and homebrew burn the back of my throat. I swallowed and tried not to throw up. We must have been a thousand feet high. The setting sun was almost covered by streaky white clouds. There were more ominous clouds ahead, and the wind was changing fast.

"Mr. Blithe, damn all, we are veering too far to the east. You must keep us on course to Springfield!" My spirits rose. Dr. Bell's voice once again had that familiar commanding tone.

Oscar shielded his eyes. "Yep, that there hill should be on our left. We are a might off course."

"How can that be? You are supposed to steer this contraption and keep us on course!"

"Well, sir, that is the thing with hot air balloons. They ain't like a horse and buggy. You can't just keep 'em right on course, especially if God don't blow wind the right direction."

"You said you would get us to Springfield."

"Well, sir, God's the pilot and we just go along for the ride. Ain't nothin' me or you or nobody else can do about it."

"And you chose not to mention this until now."

"Yes, sir. I reckoned that you being a big college professor, you already knew that, but maybe I mighta been wrong."

"Sir, our British balloonists regularly stay on course aross the English Channel," said Dr. Bell.

"This ain't no damn channel," Oscar replied.

Dark clouds crowded the horizon, dusk fell, and, suddenly, our blissful day turned ominous and cold. Dr. Bell pulled his cape coat tighter, and I wished I had mother's wool scarf.

Oscar took a long drink. "She will go down when the air in the balloon gets colder. Don't you worry none. Things are gonna be just fine. Who knows? We might even land within a few hundred miles of Springfield."

I grabbed my head in disgust. Dr. Bell harrumphed loudly.

We did drop down a ways, but, then, in the dark, it was hard knowing if we were high enough to clear the trees. We swooped over a small town and, judging from the lights, we were barely over the rooftops.

"Dang, we ain't high enough, need more hot air. I'll light her up," Oscar said.

He pulled the string. The flint and steel made a spark, but no flame.

"Damn, we must be outta gas. Probably shoulda checked that out before we lifted off."

Dr. Bell covered his face and groaned. "Aye, that would have been a good idea."

Oscar snapped the flint and pounded on the gas tank, but there was no flame. We dropped lower and lower, and, suddenly, I saw two glittery rivers just ahead. Oscar saw them, also, and hopped on one foot, then the other.

"Boys, I got good news for you. That there first river's the Mississippi and the second's the Ohio, which means that if we can clear the first and land before we hit the second, we are as good as gold."

"If?"

"Yes, sir. You see, right there between the two is the town of Cairo, Illinois. Cairo's perfect. From there, you'll easily catch a train to Springfield. So, all I gotta do is figure out how to land this thing now and make sure we don't sink in either of them there big rivers."

"You don't know how to land?" asked Dr. Bell.

"I was just joking. Of course I do. I mean . . . I just ain't never landed in the dark, ain't got that much experience. Always figured landing at night was too dangerous."

"Great God in Heaven, preserve us," Dr. Bell groaned.

A long pregnant silence hung like an ominous cloud over us. We barely breathed as we silently floated over the Mississippi. The murky water rolled on with little waves and whitecaps. Even if we landed in the water, our basket might float, but we would surely freeze.

A sudden puff of wind, pushed us to the far bank of that massive brown river and we floated over a glade of trees. "Now! Now! Now! Cut loose those sandbags if you don't want to drown in the Ohio!" Oscar shouted.

Dr. Bell opened his penknife and, with a quick slash, cut the ropes. Two sandbags fell away and we rose a few feet before settling down again. For a frightful moment, the basket touched water. Oscar cut loose two more bags. We rose twenty feet or so and glided across the Ohio River.

The wind picked up speed. We whirled through the gathering darkness with tree branches dragging at the basket. An updraft gave us another bounce for a moment, and we sailed on into the night.

I was down on the floor of the basket when Dr. Bell fell across my legs.

"Mr. Blithe, get this thing under control!" he shouted.

There was another jolt and we dragged and bumped against tree branches. Oscar sprawled across Dr. Bell and groaned. "Ain't nothing left to do. I done tried everything, but I ain't got the experience. My cousin, Lester, crashed and died in this very same basket just a month ago. Nobody in the family wanted it, so I inherited the balloon, basket, and a month's supply of gas."

I looked heavenward, but, instead of sky, saw only the crazy balloon fluttering like a half-empty sac. I hardly remember the next few seconds. Dr. Bell struggled, was almost on his feet, then fell in a heap. Oscar covered his face. "Hang on! She's gonna hit!" he shouted.

Our basket with the collapsed balloon crashed down, down through the branches of a giant tree. The gas tank struck Oscar, then we splintered wood and crashed through a roof.

The basket split in half. Oscar went flying and landed on his back, cuddling his jug like a baby. Dr. Bell was nowhere to be seen, and I was down on all fours amidst a furious flutter of wings and angry squawking. I wiped feathers out of my eyes and, when my head cleared, heard angry barking, snarling and a boy's voice in an excited shout. "PAW! PAW! THEY'S THIEVES IN THE HEN HOUSE. GIT THE GUN!"

A light went on in a farm house not thirty feet away and the back door opened. I saw an older woman who wore a long white nightgown and carried a lantern. A skinny old fellow stood in the doorway, raised a long gun, and *BOOM*!

Oscar had struggled to his feet and raised the jug, which shattered in a charge of birdshot. More pellets rattled on the chicken coop and made tree leaves go a-flutter. The shot further enraged a great snarling mastiff with bared teeth who tugged at a rusty chain.

The old fellow, his nightshirt fluttering at his knees, rammed home another charge. We were caught in the light.

I was still down, batting away a huge rooster, when Dr. Bell arose to his full six feet, two inches. His cap was askew. The two bills were over his ears and an earflap covered one eye. With his outstretched arms, his billowing cape looked for all the world like wings.

"Mon, Yir dinnae need the gun! And control yon beastie. We arna thieves, but poor fulk fallen from the heavens." I could scarcely understand Dr. Bell's Scottish burr, or why he was speaking that way, but the old lady went to her knees with hands clasped prayer.

"Oh, blessed Lord, you sent an angel from heaven!"

Dr. Bell walked towards the old lady with the measured steps of a highland lord. "Gude lady, dinnae fash yerself. We shall gladly pay for the damages to your chicken coop."

Dr. Bell held in his hand a glittering ten-dollar gold piece.

"Hallelujah, we are saved!" the woman cried. "Is that real gold?"

"From the United States mint," said Bell.

"Ma, boil up some coffee. Show these folks hospitality."

We crowded into a kitchen with a wood stove and a plank floor. The old lady set a kettle over a crackling fire and crushed coffee beans with a hammer.

I chocked down the foul, bitter brew and, once again, was glad to be alive.

Dr. Bell toyed with his cup. "Mr. Blithe, you promised to deliver us to Springfield."

"I reckon you can get a train in Cairo and be there in no time at all. I dun' pretty good considerin' the circumstances and all, and, on account of you fellers are Scotchmen, I'll reduce the charge to ten dollars. But, don't tell a soul you didn't pay the full price."

"Damn, you scoundrel, we aren't even in Cairo."

The old farmer hitched up his nightshirt and scratched a skinny leg. "If you got another one of them ten dollar pieces, I kin drive you into Cairo in time to catch the train."

"Can I go along?" Oscar asked.

"It's a deal." Dr. Bell handed over the gold coin to the aged farmer.

We piled the shredded balloon, the basket, and ourselves in wagon drawn by two balky mules and set off through brush and across fields in the direction of Cairo. I drowsed off, but jerked awake when a hoot owl screeched. Oscar claimed he saw a wolf, but, then, he had a good imagination.

It got easier when we came upon wagon tracks that, after a bit, led to a road. Finally we reached the outskirts of Cairo.

The mules ambled on the dirt road past big houses that belonged to steamboat captains and a building that Oscar said was the Customs House—which also served as a post office and courthouse.

There was not a single light or a soul on the streets. Not even a night watchman could be seen. We reached a fallen-down frame building with a porch and rocking chairs that Oscar said was a public house.

"I'm stoppin' right here. You lads go on another block to the train depot. The agent keeps the place warm," the farmer said.

We said our goodbyes and went to the cheerless depot. There was no sign of an agent, but the ancient wood-burning stove had a few glowing embers. Dr. Bell and I flopped on the floor and dozed off.

9 December, 1878

It was just light, maybe six o'clock in the morning when the Cairo stationmaster kicked my ribs with a hobnail boot. "Damn tramps. Get out of my station," he said.

"We aren't tramps," I said.

"Oh pshaw, you can't fool me. You talk like some foreigner."

Dr. Bell jumped to his feet. "Sir, we are in this country as guests of Angus Duncan who owns the railroad." He pulled out his wallet and waved a fistful of American dollars at the uncouth man. "We demand immediate transport to Springfield, and damn the expense."

"Well, this is a different story. The next train ain't due for another hour. You boys might as well go across the street and have breakfast."

Dr. Bell had toast with jam and I polished off a half-dozen fried eggs, ham, and biscuits with gravy. Bell paid a dollar and we rushed back to the station.

The agent was nowhere to be found, but Dr. Bell wrote out a telegram to warn the Pinkertons and added a note for the agent, "Urgent. Send as soon as possible," and left a gold ten dollar coin.

We paced, back and forth while Dr. Bell puffed clouds of smoke. At half nine a slow-moving goods train, with a tired wood-fired steam engine pulling two cars, chugged into the station and wheezed to a stop. The name *GLADYS* was painted in red across the boiler.

Dr. Bell hailed the engineer. "Ho, we need immediate transportation to Springfield. It is a matter of life and death. Your president is in danger."

"Ach, now. As surely as my name is Billy O'Toole I'd help you gentlemen, but ya can't fool me with a damn cock and bull story."

Billy O'Toole climbed down off the engine and ran a hand through sparse hair. I recognized a fellow Irishman by his merry eyes and red nose with broken veins. Billy clearly enjoyed a drink.

Dr. Bell took in the situation with a single glance and jingled gold coins.

"Mr. O'Toole, you will be generously rewarded and I shall put in a good word for you with Mr. Angus Duncan who owns the railroad."

"Ah, you are two pretty boys. This is a freight, don't carry no passengers. How do I know you ain't Pinkertons trying to catch me out with a bribe? My old pal, Tommy Jenkins, on the St. Louis line, lost his job when he let his drinking pals ride a freighter. I ain't gonna make the same mistake."

"Mr. O'Toole, consider our money as honest payment for passage, not a bribe. You have my word," said Dr. Bell.

"I wish I could help, but, no, sir. You can't fool me."

"Just one second. The broken blood vessels in your nose might at first appear to be windburn, but I would wager that they are telangiectasia rosacea resulting from your over-reliance on alcohol; further confirmed by the fact that even though your back pocket is empty the dye of the material is worn away in the faint outline of a flask. You drink on the job, and the pork grease under your fingernails and the scent of ham on your sleeves indicate that you are stealing cargo," said Dr. Bell.

"Well, you don't say." Billy hung his head, then came up with a sheepish smile. "Why shucks, if you boys don't mind ridin' old *Gladys* with the freight, come on board and we are on our way. You got two choices, ride with the smoked pork or sit on the grain sacks."

Dr. Bell sniffed. "Those are our only choices?"

"Yep. Now I'll fire her up and go like lightning, but we gotta cross the Big Muddy River."

"Never heard of that river," said I.

"Ain't on no map, but this time of the year she runs pretty fast, and there is so much mud the fish can't see the bait. Trouble is, the only bridge is mighty shaky. Some days, I gotta wait till the water goes down."

"We shall take that risk, sir. Sally forth," Dr. Bell replied.

The bags of grain were a might uncomfortable, but we snuggled under a canvas tarpaulin. It was not so bad. The old train did not go like lightning but, instead, puttered along at a snail's pace. It was bloody hard to be patient and then the train shuddered, clanked, sputtered, and jerked to a stop.

Billy clambered down from the cab and wiped his nose. We joined the little Irishman on the banks of a raging muddy stream. "This here is the Big Muddy River and there is the bridge."

He was right. The iron tracks were laid on a slender wooden trestles that trembled with each wave. A tree branch, rolling with the fast current, struck a wood piling. The bridge shook and creaked.

Dr. Bell opened his fine gold watch. "We must hurry on. The President's address starts in four hours. If that telegraph operator sent our message, the Pinkertons might save the President, but they will not know to look for Captain Hook. The entire country may be in dire straits."

"Aye, we are in a dire rush, but will the bridge hold?" I asked.

"*Gladys* is a heavy load, old bitch, but there's a 50/50 chance we kin make it." Billy twinkled with a crafty smile. "Now boys, let me see the color of your money."

Dr. Bell peeled off ten dollar bills. "Who was *Gladys*?" I asked.

"Yep, *Gladys*. That's what I call the old lady. Been driving her for ten years and she ain't never let me down. Named her after my schoolteacher, Miss Gladys Connors. She was one helluva woman. She used to lay my head between her thick thighs and cane my rump when I was bad."

Dr. Bell gave Billy a fist full of greenbacks. "Let us waste no more time."

"Boys. Old *Gladys* needs a head of steam. You . . ." he pointed at me. "Get up and heave wood into the boiler. We all three climbed into the engine cab.

"Yes, of course . . ." He cleared his throat. "So, as I was saying . . . *Gladys* can be mighty temperamental, and I shut her down because to get over this bridge we're going to need a full head of steam, especially considering the state of that there bridge."

Dr. Bell and I looked at the bridge. Across its entire span it seemed to be constructed of spindly timbers. And the current in the Big Muddy River swept against the wooden pilings at its base with a force that shook the entire creaky structure. It looked awfully dangerous, and I sincerely doubted that *Gladys* could traverse it safely.

Billy took a long pull at a bottle and offered me a drink. I could not say no to a fellow Irishman, so I had a long swallow, opened the furnace door, and threw chunks of wood on the fire.

"I presume you will cross the bridge slowly and with great care," said Dr. Bell.

"Hell, no, that ain't the way." The fire roared and the steam gauge topped the last red mark. Billy put her in reverse. We chugged about one hundred yards away from the bridge and came to a halt. Billy took another pull at the bottle. "Let her rip!" he yelled.

Black smoke poured out of the stack. The fire roared. Billy let off the brake and sounded the whistle. "Hold on, boys!" he whooped.

The wheels turned faster and faster until we flew. I could have sworn we left the track. *Gladys* pounded down the slope, gaining more speed until we hit the bridge. Billy kept his head out the window with one hand on the throttle. His hat flew off, but he ignored that and gave another pull on the throttle. Dr. Bell, as excited as a wee boy, yanked on the whistle. The mournful cry sounded across the little valley, but did not drown out the frightful *CRACK!* of breaking timbers.

I closed my eyes, said a good Catholic prayer, and crossed myself.

Dr. Bell did a little jig. "Aye, boys, that was grand. The grandest thing, I ever saw!"

We were across and safe. I looked back in time to see crumbling timbers and iron rails splashing in to the Big Muddy River. The bridge collapsed.

"Damn all, how am I to get home?" Billy complained. He turned obstinate, slowed at every village, tootled the whistle at every dog, child, and woman and refused to press on with more speed.

It was almost a quarter to four o'clock when we pulled into the Springfield depot. Bell anxiously consulted his watch. We had nearly fifteen minutes to save the President.

The station was deserted except for the agent, and there were no hacks, cabs or carriages.

"You will have to hoof it, but the tomb is only two miles away. The whole county's already there to hear the President," the agent said.

We set off at a brisk jog, but, after a half-mile, Dr. Bell became short of breath and slowed to a bare walk. "My dear Doyle, it is up to you. Take my revolver and run. Go, laddie, go!"

I tucked the Bull Dog pistol into my pocket and set off like a madman. I found a pace, ran well and fast, but my boots sunk into wet ground and I slipped on patches of melting snow. In a few minutes I passed latecomers and then, suddenly, saw the tall pointed obelisk of Lincoln's tomb where I heard snatches of a stentorian voice.

Damn it all to bloody hell! Hayes had started early. Was I too late?

From a distance, I saw four flights of balustraded stairs—two flanking the entrance and two at the rear. Both led to a level terrace where the President stood in front of an ornate parapet. Patriotic red, white, and blue banners and streamers fluttered from flag poles. Dignitaries surrounded the President. I was uplifted by the display and paused to listen. Hayes, in full throat, waved his arms. "We are gathered today to honour the saviour of our union—" he roared.

Stern-faced Pinkertons with rifles at the ready were on guard. They stood in front of the tomb and on the balustrade looking out over the crowd. They were intent on protecting the President and seemed competent. Things appeared to be in order with nothing amiss.

I breathed a sigh of relief. The Pinkertons were on the job, and, besides, the country folks and city people were purely innocent.

I looked around the cemetery and saw people stretched as far as the eye could see. There had to be a few thousand spectators spread out on the grassy lawn in front of the tomb, on the steps, the terrace, the balustrade. A few young bucks had climbed the bronze statues for a better view. Far in the back, folks listened from open carriages.

President Hayes must be popular because people clapped and hurrahed. Enthusiasm was in the air. Venders wandered among the crowd hawking peanuts and beer.

Children played tag in the mud. There were picnic hampers, and young couples held hands. Even though the day was overcast, it was more like a jolly holiday than a national event. Her Majesty, Queen Victoria, would not allow such nonsense.

I pushed through the crowds on the lookout for Captain Hook, especially beneath the terrace because Emilie Droussard had said "below the tomb."

Nothing looked suspicious. All was festive. Did Bell's telegram get through? Perhaps the Pinkertons had already found Hook and his accomplices.

I began to relax and idly listen to President Hayes, when someone brushed my shoulder. "Well, lad, have you observed anything of note?" It was Dr. Bell.

"No, sir."

"Perhaps I was mistaken and there is nothing to fear," he said.

The clouds parted for a moment, and I had to squint to see over the crowd towards the west. "Sir, look over yonder. What a gallant band of horsemen. They must be farmers, late arrivals." The band came on at a brisk trot. I counted twenty or more men riding two abreast.

Dr. Bell shielded his eyes. "How curious; they are accompanied by two large wagons and seem to be riding with purpose. Doyle, do you recognize those types of wagons?"

"If I am not mistaken, they are the great Conestoga wagons used to carry settlers west to California. The first appears to have a load of baled hay," I said.

The wagons were a hundred yards away when the wheels sunk into a patch of deep mud. The drivers whipped up the struggling animals with cries of "Gee up!"

Four massive draft horses were hitched to each wagon, but the wagon wheels appeared to be stuck. The horses struggled forward and pulled the wagons to drier ground. One wagon came to the last row of spectators. The other dashed onto a small knoll in the back of the cemetery.

Bell was suddenly alert. His eyes twinkled as if he were in the amphitheatre solving a ticklish clinical problem. "Doyle, my lad, observe those horses. They are under great strain. They sweat and are well-lathered. Their nostrils flare and, man, look at those deep ruts left in the mud. There is more than hay in those wagons. What do you deduce from these observations?"

"They carry a heavy load, especially the wagon moving towards the knoll. But, sir, they are only farmers," said I.

"Doyle, those men are no ordinary farmers. They are expert horsemen."

"Yes, yes, of course. They wear slouch hats and peculiar long coats. Perhaps they are cowboys," I said.

"Doyle, use your head. Those coats are dusters, perfect to conceal weapons. They ride like cavalry men." Bell sniffed the air like a bloodhound and slapped his head. "Damn it! I smell gun oil. Those men are heavily armed. I was wrong. Droussard's last message was not *below the tomb*, but *BLOW THE TOMB!*"

"Bloody hell!" I exclaimed.

"Follow me!" he shouted, and set off at a run towards the nearest wagon.

President Hayes made a rousing statement. Amidst the cheers one wagon halted on a shallow decline almost in the midst of the spectators. The other continued to slowly move forward and came to a halt.

We were within a few feet of the first wagon when the driver threw down the reins and pulled off his long coat. The uniform was old and patched, but unmistakably Confederate cavalry. The man was a veteran of many a campaign. He was a hard, grizzled-looking man who wore sergeant's stripes.

At his side, in a brown scabbard, was a long, deadly sabre. He paused and puffed hard until the cigar jammed between his teeth glowed brightly. With frantic haste, he tore away the canvas covering and hurled bales of hay from the wagon to reveal wooden crates marked 'US ARMORY'.

With a long knife, he tore open one crate in the middle of the pile to reveal bundles of red sticks. The wagon was filled with dynamite, enough to blow up the monument and kill the president and thousands of innocent people. The confederate jammed a long fuse between sticks of dynamite, jumped from the wagon, and unrolled the fuse as he went.

Nobody, not one of that crowd, noticed. Folks whistled, shouted, and roared with applause at the President's speech. The noise was deafening.

"Somebody, stop that man! Stop him!" I waved my arms and tried to attract attention.

It was no use. I jerked my head at the sound of pounding hoofbeats. There, not twenty feet away, a fellow on a chestnut horse coolly took aim and fired his Winchester at me. I ducked, stumbled, and fell face down. The bullet made a small geyser in the soft mud by my face. I was up and running again, with bullets whistling in the air. Dr. Bell saw my plight. He was closer to the wagon and there was no way I could get there in time. With a burst of speed, he dodged the whistling bullets and reached the wagon just as the sergeant put his cigar to the fuse.

The fuse sizzled and sparked. The enraged sergeant drew his sabre and swung the steel blade in a deadly arc. Bell ducked and, with one motion, pulled out his meerschaum pipe and smashed the heavy bowl on the man's temple. The sergeant went down. In an instant Dr. Bell snatched the sabre and sliced the burning fuse with all the élan of a clansmen in Bonny Prince Charlie's army. Bell then jerked the remaining fuse away from the dynamite.

He had done it. Dr. Bell had saved the day.

The now-shortened fuse spluttered out into thin air and the dynamite sat silently in its box with an unlit squat fuse.

I ran towards the wagon to congratulate him, but, before we could celebrate, one of the other horsemen riding a big chestnut stallion at full tilt, dashed towards us. His whip stung my shoulder as he passed. "Damn you both! Get out of the way!" he shouted. My attacker rode like an old veteran, a cavalryman. I realized, with a horrible certainty, that these men were hard core survivors of Nathan Bedford Forrest's troops. These were the villains we had been searching for across America.

As I leaped away from the next strike of his whip, I noticed that the other wagon driver had moved again and parked his four-wheeled cart behind some trees on top of the knoll overlooking the crowd and the tomb. That driver then jumped into the back of his wagon, tossing the hay off the wagon and onto the ground.

As he did, he began to expose a most distressing sight. Under the bales of hay was a large canvas which, when ripped away, revealed the big, ugly snout of an artillery piece aimed directly at the tomb.

I had studied military weaponry at university and knew that a cannon of that size could send twelve-inch shells hundreds of yards in the air. If a shell of that calibre struck the tomb, the entire structure would surely collapse, killing hundreds of people.

"Doyle, the revolver! Use the revolver!" Dr. Bell yelled, as President Hayes paused between phrases.

I heard him, but so did everybody else nearby, and bedlam ensued.

The riders on now-frenzied, bucking horses dashed in a great circle while throwing off their long coats. Each one had a pistol in their belt and a repeating Winchester rifle in hand. Every man wore either a faded Confederate uniform or a red shirt. "Sic Semper Tyrannis! Long Live the South!" they shouted.

The crowd took notice and, though many people screamed and began running in different directions, some simply laughed and clapped as if this were another Wild West show.

The riders created a diversion with their shooting and shouting. Dr. Bell, with his long legs pumping, was on a mad, limping run towards the second wagon.

By now, I had the revolver out of my pocket and, with great leaping strides, ran towards the deadly cannon. The officer, in the gaudy uniform of a major general, lit a match and leaned over the touch hole of the beastly cannon.

I was yards away when Bell shouted. "Doyle, for God's sake, shoot!"

I had no experience with fire arms, but, with trembling hands, I pulled back the hammer and pressed the trigger. I missed, fired, and missed again. At the sound of my revolver, the Southern officer paused long enough for Dr. Bell to reach the lead horse in the team. He grasped the halter and pulled. The horse balked, but, with frantic effort, the good doctor hung on for dear life. He turned the horses head. The team reacted to the lead horse. They pulled as if one animal and jerked the wagon into a sudden motion. The general lost his balance and dropped the match. He fumbled in his pocket for another. The wagon made a quarter turn. He struck a flame and ignited a few grains of powder in the touch hole.

I watched, horrified. The cannon roared and shot flames. The great *BOOM!* rocked me back. The shell flew, but not at Lincoln's tomb. Miraculously, the shell crashed and exploded harmlessly in the cemetery to the north. Headstones, earth, and trees erupted in a great geyser, but no one was hurt. Dr. Bell had succeeded in turning the wagon away from its target. The President was safe.

My first thought was for Dr. Bell. Had he been in the path of the shell?

When I saw him, he was flat on his face, but unhurt. I breathed a sigh of relief when he opened his eyes.

The Pinkertons came at a run and roughly shackled the old major general. The Confederates fired wildly and charged through the crowd. When two of their riders fell, killed by the Pinkerton's intense fire, they hesitated, then galloped away. More than one farmer in the crowd blazed away with squirrel rifles and shotguns.

The undaunted President resumed his long speech. "Please, fellow citizens. The danger has passed. Let us forgive our Southern brothers—"

The people—all those farmers, city folk, veterans, and children, now stunned into silence—edged in closer with renewed interest in the President's words. Meanwhile, the Pinkertons and volunteers helped the injured into makeshift ambulances.

Among the gaping, church-quiet audience I had lost track of Dr. Bell. Along with the others, I made my way closer to the tomb and rather idly noticed a poor elderly man with a white cane. He wore a black hat pulled low over his face and a brown coat, with long, ill-fitting sleeves that hung well below his wrists. I assumed he was a sad, blinded veteran of The Great War, perhaps injured at Shiloh or Gettysburg.

He stumbled, and my heart went out to him. He tapped his cane and limped a short distance towards the memorial. People stepped aside and made way for his deliberate progress. He stopped, pulled his dirty beard, and seemed to be listening to the President. He went on, slowly, but always towards the President, as if he wanted to be closer. Perhaps he was deaf as well as blind. Still, I took a closer look.

Something was not quite right, but I could not put my finger on it. The cane was brand new. The handle was unusual, too intricate for a poor man's cane. I instantly thought of Dr. Bell's *sword cane*. No, the idea was preposterous. I could not let my imagination run wild.

President Hayes went on. "This is a great era, a time for forgiveness. Let us seek peace with our Southern brothers . . ."

The tap, tap on the marble staircase continued. The blind man was almost on the terrace behind the President when he stopped and cocked his head as if listening. I assumed the poor man was a disoriented or confused veteran. A Pinkerton guard watched him briefly, then looked away across the crowded field.

The fellow moved on, deliberately now. For the first time, he raised the tip of the cane as a blind man will do if searching for an obstacle. It seemed to be a perfectly normal gesture. At that instant, the clouds parted, and bright sunshine flooded the terrace. It was as if God had shed a beam on the President to bless his salvation from the would-be assassins.

The shaft of sunlight reflected off bright metal at the tip of the cane. Why was there suddenly new metal on the cane? Instantly, the pieces of the puzzle fell into place. I envisioned with great clarity the puncture wounds of the curare victims. The so-called blind man had pressed a button in the head of the cane and flicked out what I knew was a deadly needle. I was sure he was preparing to kill the President.

Even with that clarity of thought, I could not fully believe it until the man stopped his hesitant tapping and lunged towards the President. I watched, mouth open, but could make no sound. I was paralyzed with inaction. Where was Doctor Bell? I felt worthless until, suddenly, I came to my senses and saw the blind man's right sleeve had ridden up his arm a bit, revealing a hook instead of a hand. It was him. Captain Spencer, better known as Captain Hook.

My heart was pounding. Panic filled my mind. But, I had to act immediately. At that point, it was not about me, or my drunken father, or anything else in the world, except saving lives. I heard Dr. Bell's voice in my head and all he had taught me about using my mind to uncover the truth and then act on it. I had overcome enough obstacles over these few days and had survived each one. I knew I could do this. I knew I had to do this.

"Damn you! Captain Spencer, HALT!" I screamed, as loudly as I could. I drew the pistol, aimed, and pulled the trigger. There was only a sharp click.

The President, alerted by my frantic cry, stopped in mid-sentence, and, with unsuspected agility, dodged to one side. The deadly can missed the President.

Hook turned his eyes, murderous with hatred, on me. His face twisted. "You again? Damn you, boy!" He lunged at me with the cane held point-first. "Justice! Down with the tyrannical North!" he shouted.

Before he could attempt to attack the President again, I made a flying tackle, hit his knees, and felt his hook swipe across the top of my head. I rolled and smashed a fist into his groin. The hook slashed across my cheek. I made a terrific kick that snapped his femur. We rolled together down the steps.

The man was incredibly strong and was able to keep going despite any pain in his groin and leg. I rolled onto my back and there, above me, he was poised to plunge the tip of his cane into my neck. I heaved him away and rolled down one step. Like a tiger, he was upon me again, but, this time, I grabbed his arm, and, with all my might, forced the poisoned cane away from my body. He held onto the cane and attempted to rise, but I kicked his broken leg. He crumpled, and the deadly tip entered his stomach. The curare worked its way through his body. He had impaled himself with his own deadly weapon.

In his last paroxysm, his mouth opened, and his tongue moved, but he could not utter a word. He went limp, took his last breath, and died, practically in my arms. His death came surprisingly quick. I supposed it was because he had loaded the cane with an extra strong dose of the poison to kill the President. His eyes had the same pleading look I had seen in Carl and the poor rat.

I expected immediate accolades, but, much to my amazement, the opposite was true. "That's him! He tried to shoot the President!" cried the gathering crowd. A half-dozen Pinkertons pinned me down, applied steel shackles to my hands and feet, and dragged me away to a barred police wagon.

The cries hushed. President Hayes made a last comment about forgiving the South before his guards hurried him away to a place of safety. The Pinkertons roughly tossed me into the police wagon, on my way to a prison cell.

When we arrived at the police station about twenty minutes later, the guards dragged me inside while a crowd gathered outside. "Lynch the damn bastard! Kill the assassin!"

While the crowd screamed for my blood, the guards threw me face down onto the floor of a filthy, solitary cell. I was still shackled and beset by an angry mob. Where was justice? What a damnable country. I risked my life to save the President and my reward was to have the entire populace of Springfield wanting to hang me.

Where was Dr. Bell? Was he, too, under suspicion? It wasn't until later that I learned he had gone off to send an urgent telegram to Angus Duncan. He searched for me, not realizing I was in a dirty cell.

I remember that long, dreadful night. My hand still trembles as I write these words. On that cold stone floor, amidst pools of filth and chittering rats, I vowed to give up travel and adventure and settle in dear old Scotland to practise medicine and, who knows, maybe even write.

10 December, 1878

It was almost noon before the authorities identified Captain Spencer, a.k.a. Captain Hook, and later still before Dr. Bell, with the aid of Angus Duncan, came to my rescue. I was never so glad to see his dear homely face.

Dr. Bell put out a hand, ignoring my mud and filth-covered fingers. "Come now, laddie, you must be famished. Join us for a wee dram and meal."

"Aye, sir. Aye."

The lynch mob had dispersed, the railroads were cleared, and Mr. Duncan's personal gilded railroad carriage waited to take us back to Chicago.

As we sat in the luxury of Duncan's private carriage a fierce northeast wind blew gusts of snow against the windows. The carriage creaked with the cold, but a crackling blaze in an iron stove warmed my bones. Our belongings were still in the Peabody Hotel, but Mr. Duncan shared warm clothing and provided a fine meerschaum pipe for my use. Its fragrant smoky aroma filled the air and, in between puffs, we imbibed hot toddies, ate fresh oysters, boiled shrimp, and a strange soup, gumbo, fresh from New Orleans.

After I could eat no more Mr. Duncan and Dr. Bell relaxed with drinks and read the latest newspapers. I selected a Herman Melville novel, *Moby Dick,* from Mr. Duncan's library and settled down in a soft armchair to read about the adventures of Ahab.

A few moments later, Mr. Duncan laid down his pipe and newspaper. "I am sorry to say, gentlemen, but the newspapers make no mention of your adventure. There is nothing to corroborate your story. I am especially doubtful of your ludicrous tale riding in a balloon."

"The agent in Cairo and the President's guards will surely confirm our story," I instantly replied.

"Ah my dear Doyle, you do not understand. The station agent and the train driver will deny us to their deathbed for fear they will be accused of taking bribes. The Pinkertons are so humiliated by their inability to protect the President that they have hushed up the entire episode. The American public will never know how a couple of foreign sawbones saved their President," said Doctor Bell.

"How do they explain the explosives, the cannon, the armed men, or Captain Hook?"

"The Pinkertons claimed it was all good fun by a band of rowdies to celebrate the President's visit. The Americans fire guns and cannons just for fun. The crowd trampled Captain Spencer's body. The President was led to believe he was a harmless, poor old veteran."

"How can they obscure the truth?" I asked. "Uch, it makes no difference. Someday, I shall put it all in a book for the world to read so they will know what REALLY happened."

Duncan made a face, as if he had swallowed a sour pickle. "Mr. Doyle, you are a fine young man. Calm yourself. Would England admit that a couple of Americans, including one who is practically a boy, thwarted a plot to kill the Queen?"

That bit of repartee left me at a loss. Dr. Bell winked, put down his glass, and picked up a leather-bound book. "Angus, if you desire confirmation of our story, listen as I read from Emilie Droussard's casebook. She gave it to me as she lay dying."

Dr. Bell flipped through its pages. "The first part is mostly a diary starting at the beginning of the war. She learned the fundamentals of medicine from her father, a prominent New Orleans physician, but gave up hopes of becoming a doctor when she married a dashing officer. General Butler executed her father on a charge of treason and a Union sniper killed her husband at Vicksburg."

"Clearly, she had good cause to hate the North," murmured Duncan.

"She became a spy for Nathan Bedford Forrest and, with her elegant good looks, she had access to Union officers in the border states. She passed secrets through Dr. McGillicutty, a Rebel surgeon who introduced her to Captain Andrew Spencer, one of Forrest's men. She, in fact, assisted McGillicutty when Spencer lost his hand. This re-kindled her interest in medicine, but, after the war, every medical school in America refused her admission."

"Women have no place in medicine," said Angus.

I disagreed, but did not argue the point.

Dr. Bell ignored him and continued. "She gained admission to a medical school in Switzerland and, there, she again met Dr. McGillicutty who developed an intense interest in the implantation of monkey glands to rejuvenate ill, old men. McGillicutty was far ahead of his time. His work with grafting skin to the victims of the Chicago Fire was outstanding, but unappreciated. His determination to carry on led him to the remote scarlet house in Sherlock, which was the only place he could do his experiments in peace."

"All that makes sense. But, so far, you have told us nothing of a conspiracy to restore the Confederacy," said Angus.

"I was getting to that. Captain Spencer, or, as he was so aptly called, Captain Hook, never surrendered. The government charged him with murder because of his involvement at Fort Pillow and would have had him hanged. Instead, he ran to Mexico, joined Maximilian's army, and later fled to South America."

"Yes, many Confederates fled rather than live under the Union," Angus added.

"Spencer was driven by a lust for revenge. He made a fortune in gold mines and, incidentally, collected a large amount of the curare poison from the natives. He returned to this country, but, like so many other veterans, was in failing health. That is how he came to be re-united with Emilie Droussard and Dr. McGillicutty."

"Then, I <u>was</u> correct. McGillicutty was involved," said I.

"Yes, McGillicutty's experiments failed because of his difficulties in anaesthetizing the animals. The monkeys became wild and dangerous. He could not find a dose that would allow the animals to live and yet keep them paralyzed for the surgery. Emilie conceived of administering the drug with a syringe attached to a long pole placed through the cages. That, of course, led to the poison cane that killed, silently, from a safe distance."

"Wait. When did they start to work on human subjects?" I asked.

"Well, at first they gave liquid extracts of the glands to Captain Spencer. Here is a quote from her casebook. *'20 minims aqueous extract of a monkey's thyroid gland injected into the Captain.'* A second notation one week later read, *'Captain is agitated, pulse 120, no improvement in physical condition.'* This failure led to further experiments with human glands."

Mr. Duncan took a long drink of this toddy. "Again, I regret saying this, but this whole plot sounds rather hard to swallow." He spluttered on his drink and had a long coughing spell.

"I know. It is representative of the horror of medical science sans ethics. For example, here is a description of their first 'specimen'. '*Male schoolteacher, carpetbagger, aged twenty-two years. Paralyzed with curare, thyroid gland removed while specimen still alive. Extract injected into Captain Spencer. Improved.*'"

"Was McGillicutty involved at this point?" I asked.

"No, Doyle. He objected to using humans and abandoned the project, but, Hook, with his renewed energy, commenced recruiting men for his rebel army. His efforts led him to Chicago. There, according to Droussard, is where they hit upon the plan to use railroad guards as their specimens. The men were all young and strong. In addition, their loss would weaken the railroad's security and allow for their ultimate attack on the United States government."

"Diabolical. I feel awful about my poor men. I must set up a fund to help their families," Angus murmured. "Well, gentlemen, I do apologize. Sorry for ever doubting your story."

"Good . . . Then, we shall be in need of this no longer." Dr. Bell snapped the casebook closed, walked to the fireplace and, with a puff of his pipe, dropped the book in the flames.

The pages caught fire. Maybe it was all for the best to spare the country from another dreadful story of rebellion. For now, it was best to allow healing. Perhaps I should even destroy my own journal. I lacked heart, but promised myself that this journal would never see the light of day while I lived. Our exploits, and the American adventure, would forever remain a secret.

"Arthur Doyle. Mr. Arthur Conan Doyle?" We had just disembarked from our coach as the porter shouted my name.

I lifted my arm, "Aye, that's me."

The porter handed me a telegram from Carl.

Rufus is better. I must lean on Rebecca to walk any distance, but we sometimes go to the river and think of you. Jimmy is fine. We shall return to Rush, but you will be gone. Please write to us when you are home.

The telegram mentioned nothing of marriage, but deep in my heart I know Carl and Rebecca are meant for each other. I was pondering this thought when we reached Mr. Duncan's mansion. "Laddie, you did me proud. But, I am curious . . ." Dr. Bell paused to sip from a glass of golden single malt whisky. "How did you know the assassin was Captain Hook?" he asked.

"It is rather elementary," said I. "My dear Doctor Bell, it was a great surgeon who taught me to observe and deduce in order to make the proper diagnosis."

With that, I lay down my pen and close this diary.

~ Arthur Conan Doyle, student.

Sir Arthur Conan Doyle once said, "It is a capital mistake to theorize before one has data." And so, my dear reader, before you close this extraordinary manuscript discovered by my colleague, Dr. John Raffensperger, there are some historical facts that I believe you should know about the actual life of the real Arthur Conan Doyle, et. al.

Fact. Arthur Conan Doyle embarked on his medical studies at the University of Edinburgh in 1876 when he was nineteen and Edinburgh was the world's center for medical education and surgery. The university was renowned for its curriculum, which included studies of the humanities as well as science. Joseph Lister had transformed surgical practise with his discovery of antisepsis that banished infection from wounds and was the world-famous professor of surgery.

Fact. The impoverished Arthur Conan Doyle barely had the admitting tuition and was forced to periodically support himself as a ship's surgeon or an assistant to country doctors. He also earned money by writing short stories. In 1878, one of his professors, Dr. Joseph Bell, appointed Doyle to be his outpatient clerk.

Fact. Dr. Bell had contracted diphtheria from a patient while he was a house surgeon. The disease affected his vocal cords and his gait but did not prevent him from becoming one of the foremost surgeons in Scotland. In addition to teaching students and running his large personal practice, Dr. Bell wrote textbooks, edited medical journals, and was the secretary-treasurer of the Royal College of Surgeons. Bell was especially gentle with children and, when his term at the Royal Infirmary expired, he became the first surgeon to have a ward at the Royal Edinburgh Children's Hospital where he continued to operate and teach.

Fact. Bell could deduce a patient's occupation, nationality and place of origin from such details as the calluses on their hands, mud on their boots and their accent. With his uncanny powers of observation he made rapid and accurate medical diagnoses. In the position of clerk to Dr. Bell, Arthur Conan Doyle briefly examined new patients to make a preliminary diagnosis. He then presented the patient to Dr. Bell in the great amphitheatre of the Edinburgh Infirmary in front of medical students and house officers.

Fact. When Doyle became his clerk, Dr. Bell was 36 years old, sparse, lean and tall with an aquiline nose and black hair. He had long sensitive fingers; his gray eyes twinkled with shrewdness. This is almost the exact same description that Dr. Watson made of Sherlock Holmes during their first meeting at 221B Baker Street in *A Study In Scarlet*. Indeed, Conan Doyle ultimately confirmed that Dr. Joseph Bell was his model for the great detective.

Fact. The esteemed authors Robert Louis Stevenson and James Barrie were real-life contemporaries and colleagues of Doyle at Edinburgh University.

And so, just as we began this endnote, let us also end with words of our esteemed hero, the real Sir Arthur Conan Doyle. *"How often have I said to you that when you have eliminated the impossible, whatever remains, however improbable, must be the truth?"*

~ Prof. Richard Krevolin, Los Angeles, CA. 11:41 a.m., February 29, 2016.

About The Authors

Dr. John Raffensperger, a retired pediatric surgeon, read all of the Sherlock Holmes stories as a child, and by the age of twelve, was convinced that Basil Rathbone was the real great detective. Years later, he discovered that Dr. Joe Bell, the 'real' Sherlock Holmes, had been the first pediatric surgeon at the Royal Edinburgh Children's Hospital. This led to an interest in the role that Dr. Bell played in the life of Arthur Conan Doyle. Dr. Raff is a medical historian who has written medical articles, textbooks of surgery, a history of pediatric surgery, sailing stories, and three novels. He now lives on an island off the coast of Florida and is training a hound, Daisy, to howl on moonless nights.

Prof. Richard Krevolin was thrilled when Dr. Raffensperger brought him the only existing copy of the lost journals of Sir Arthur Conan Doyle. He spent the next few years editing them, and when he's not editing he can be found solving murder mysteries, writing plays, consulting, teaching, and directing films. He is a graduate of Yale College and has several graduate degrees. Krevolin now lives deep in the San Fernando Valley where he can be found oil painting. More info about him can be found at www.ProfK.com & www.PowerStoryConsulting.com

Also from MX Publishing

MX Publishing is the world's largest specialist Sherlock Holmes publisher, with over a hundred titles and fifty authors creating the latest in Sherlock Holmes fiction and non-fiction.

From traditional short stories and novels to travel guides and quiz books, MX Publishing caters to all Holmes fans.

The collection includes leading titles such as *Benedict Cumberbatch In Transition* and *The Norwood Author* which won the 2011 Howlett Award (Sherlock Holmes Book of the Year).

MX Publishing also has one of the largest communities of Holmes fans on Facebook with regular contributions from dozens of authors.

www.mxpublishing.com

Also from MX Publishing

 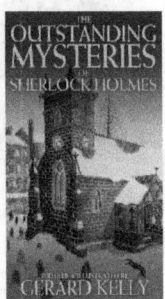

Our bestselling short story collections 'Lost Stories of Sherlock Holmes', 'The Outstanding Mysteries of Sherlock Holmes', 'Untold Adventures of Sherlock Holmes' (and the sequel 'Studies in Legacy') and 'Sherlock Holmes in Pursuit'.

 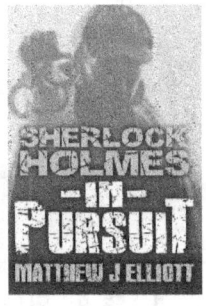

Also from MX Publishing

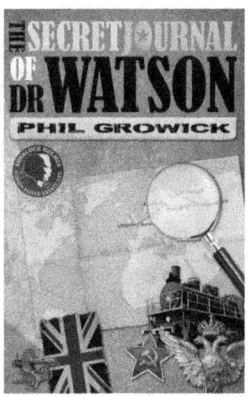

"Phil Growick's, *'The Secret Journal of Dr Watson'*, is an adventure which takes place in the latter part of Holmes and Watson's lives. They are entrusted by HM Government (although not officially) and the King no less to undertake a rescue mission to save the Romanovs, Russia's Royal family, from a grisly end at the hand of the Bolsheviks. There is a wealth of detail in the story but not so much as would detract us from the enjoyment of the story. Espionage, counter-espionage, the ace of spies himself, double-agents, double-crossers . . . all these flit across the pages in a realistic and exciting way. All the characters are extremely well-drawn and Mr Growick, most importantly, does not falter with a very good ear for Holmesian dialogue indeed. Highly recommended. A five-star effort."

The Baker Street Society

The characters return in the sequel, *The Revenge of Sherlock Holmes.*

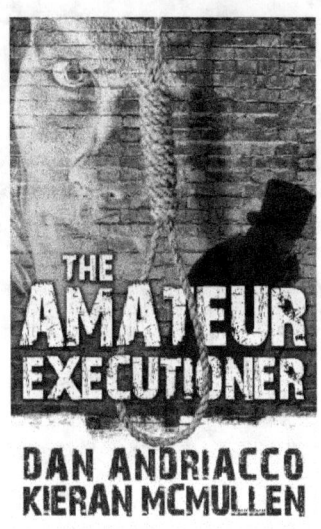

London, 1920: Boston-bred Enoch Hale, working as a reporter for the Central Press Syndicate, arrives on the scene shortly after a music hall escape artist is found hanging from the ceiling in his dressing room. What at first appears to be a suicide turns out to be murder . . .

The Enoch Hale and Sherlock Holmes series continues with *The Poisoned Penman* and concludes with *The Egyptian Curse*.

This series brings together two of the most prolific Sherlock Holmes writers of their era – Dan Andriacco and Kieran McMullen.